AF154468

David Van Horne

The Mountain Boy of Wildhaus

.

David Van Horne

The Mountain Boy of Wildhaus

ISBN/EAN: 9783744670821

Printed in Europe, USA, Canada, Australia, Japan

Cover: Foto ©Raphael Reischuk / pixelio.de

More available books at **www.hansebooks.com**

THE

MOUNTAIN BOY

OF

WILDHAUS.

A Life of Ulric Zwingli.

BY REV. DAVID VAN HORNE, D.D.

PHILADELPHIA:
REFORMED CHURCH PUBLICATION BOARD,
907 ARCH STREET.
1884.

COPYRIGHT

BY REV. DAVID VAN HORNE.

1884.

PREFACE.

THE four hundredth anniversary of the birth-day of Ulric Zwingli, which occurs on January 1st, 1884, is the immediate occasion for the preparation of this volume. Independent of this fact, however, the life of Zwingli is worthy of careful study; for although many nobles and princes of his times are now forgotten, the Mountain Boy of Wildhaus still maintains a prominent place in history. His is a life which will command attention, and will be more appreciated as men devote themselves to its study.

In the following pages attention is especially given to the events of the earlier years of his life, in the hope of interesting the young. We trust that this class of readers will find pleasure, and profit, in following the career of one who began life in a humble station, and attained an eminence in the world of letters, equalled only by the signal services he rendered to his native country, and the extensive work he wrought for the reformation of the church. In each aspect of his life Zwingli presents a bold and striking figure, well calculated to arrest the attention of American youth; and one withal, from the study of which, they can gain inspiration for future effort. There was a lofty, intrepid, and noble spirit planted in this Swiss youth, which always brought him in the fore-front of every conflict, and rendered his career one of incident and danger.

The recent celebration of the anniversary of Luther's birth-day will naturally suggest a comparison between the

3

two Reformers. The cause of the Reformation of the sixteenth century, in which both Luther and Zwingli labored co-ordinately, and, at the first, without any knowledge of each other's views and efforts, sheds a great lustre upon their works and characters. So far from appearing as rivals, they are to be regarded as co-workers in a common cause. Each one worked in his own way, and, by study and prayer, reached his own conclusion. Luther stood forth prominently as the Reformer of Germany, a nation with extensive historic connections, which afforded him the support of Electors and Princes, and speedily spread abroad his fame in other countries.

Zwingli's field of operation, on the other hand, was confined chiefly to Switzerland, his native country; he had only the town-council of Zurich, to defend him, while, for many years, his powerful enemies lay in wait to cut him off. Under these circumstances, the extensive work wrought by the great Swiss Reformer, appears the more remarkable and praiseworthy. Protestantism owes him a greater debt than it has ever yet acknowledged; and hereafter when men begin to search for the first beginnings of a pure Reformed doctrine, and the cultus of nearly the whole Protestant church, they will be led to wonder how it was that the pastor of Zurich anticipated what the future generations would adopt as the restored form of primitive Christianity.

PHILADELPHIA, January 1st, 1884.

CONTENTS.

5

CHAPTER VIII.

CHAPTER IX.

CHAPTER X.

CHAPTER XI.

CHAPTER XII.

CHAPTER XIII.

CHAPTER XIV.

CHAPTER XV.

CHAPTER XVI.

THE MOUNTAIN BOY

OF

WILDHAUS.

A LIFE OF ULRIC ZWINGLI.

CHAPTER I.

WILDHAUS.

NEAR the source of the majestic river, called by the Swiss and German people, "Father Rhine," there still stands a primitive-looking structure, perched against a spur of Mt. Sentis, known as the home of Zwingli. It is a plain but massive building, erected evidently for endurance, and intended as a safe shelter from the roaring Alpine winds which, during the long winter nights, sweep over the place. And here this ancient-looking dwelling has maintained its position, during the long, and eventful, years which have transpired since the days when a bright and promising boy played there nearly four hundred years ago. The building doubtless has been renewed many times; meanwhile the origi-

7

nal timbers may have all fallen into decay, and yet the identity of the structure remains, the same general aspect has been preserved, and to this day it is called by the name of Zwingli.

Not far away from this ancient structure the traveler may see the church-spires of the little village of Wildhaus. This village is rightly named; for it is a "Wild-house" indeed. Situated far up among the rugged Alps, on the water-shed which divides the waters of the Thur from those of the Rhine, it presents a bold figure in the landscape. Every year many tourists pass through Wildhaus, all of whom are charmed with its mountain prospects, and linger, with pleasure, around the place where the Alp scenery is so magnificent.

Before we trace the interesting career of the subject of our sketch, let us tarry, for a few moments, here to view the place of his birth. Wildhaus has a sightly situation, and we may be enabled to gain new views of our subject by glancing at its environment. First of all we notice the magnificent mountain called Sentis. This is now in the direct route of modern tourists, and therefore we can well afford to give it more than passing notice. Sentis stands just to the north of Wildhaus, and as it rears its snow-

crowned head 8,000 feet above the level of the
sea, appears like an ancient sentinel keeping
guard over the little village, which clings, like
an eagle's nest, to its southern slope. From the
summit of Sentis one may look over the greater
part of north-east and east Switzerland; em-
bracing the lake of Constance, Swabia and Bavaria, the Tyrolese mountains, the Grisons, and
the Alps of Glarus, and of Bern. Just behind
the mountain, on the north, lies St. Gaul; where,
in former times, was a noted monastery named
after its founder; who was, according to tradition, originally a missionary from Scotland, or
the north of Ireland. He came into this region
of country when the whole of Switzerland was
a wilderness inhabited by the rude ancestors of
the Swiss and Germans, who, before this, were
idolaters; and to whom he taught the truths of
the Christian religion.

It was the seventh century when St. Gaul, in
company with the missionary Columban, first
appeared in the country.

Both missionaries labored together in another
part of Switzerland for some time, but when,
afterward, persecutions arose against their work,
Columban went to Italy and labored there. But
St. Gaul resolved to continue, and for this pur-

pose came into the region of country surrounding Mt. Sentis, and, in company with a deacon
named Hiltibad, searched for a suitable location
in which to establish a mission. At the first
Hiltibad was fearful that their work would be
in vain; and warned the missionary that he
would be in constant danger, for the forests were
filled with wolves and bears. But St. Gaul only
replied: "If the Lord be for us who can be
against us? He who protected Daniel, when he
was in the lion's den, will surely protect me."
The two then traveled on together until they
came to a place where the river Steinach, as
it rushed down from the mountain heights, had
hollowed out a deep place, abounding in fish.
Here the good deacon, in imitation of the early
disciples, cast in his net, and obtained an abundant supply of the finny tribe. It was at this
place that St. Gaul then resolved to center his
work for the cause of God; and here, afterwards,
sprang up the monastery which lasted for many
centuries, bearing the name of its famous founder.
Standing still upon the summit of Sentis we
can see the waters of the lake of Constance behind St. Gaul; and far beyond, in the north-
east, may be seen the white peaks of the Tyrolese mountains.

Turning now to the north, and west, we may see the beautiful valley of the Toggenburg, down which rushes the rapid Thur. And at the head of the valley, beside the springs which are its perennial source, clinging, as it were, to the side of old Sentis, stands the cottage in which we are now specially interested, where Zwingli was born. Looking beyond this point, only a few miles farther towards the southwest, we note the tranquil waters of the lake of Wallenstadt, or " Wallensee," as it was formerly called. It is twelve miles in length and three in width ; at the east end of it lies the village of Wallenstadt, and at the west end stands the beautiful town of Wesen, also famous in Reformation circles, in after times. Still farther northward, and over fifty miles from Wildhaus, stands the stately city of Zurich, where Zwingli in after years wrought his greatest work of reformation. A little to the south of this, and across the lake of Zurich, stands Einsiedeln, another point made famous by the early labors of Zwingli. And still farther away, on the horizon of the south-west, lie the cities of Bern and Basel, where Zwingli once pursued his studies.

We only add that to the eastward, a few miles distant from Wildhaus, flow swiftly onward the clear blue waters of the upper Rhine.

Thus we notice that the location of our little village is very picturesque and charming. Perched upon the southern face of a lofty mountain, which rears its snow-clad summit against the blue Alpine sky; with chains of lakes and running streams so connected as to form a vast surrounding triangle; reaching from Zurich on the west by the way of the Zurich and Wallenstadt lakes, to the river Rhine on the east; thence to the lake of Constance on the northeast, and by another reach of the Rhine back again to Zurich. This vast triangular section of country, framed about with lakes of the utmost picturesqueness and beauty, tied together with silver-threaded rivulets; with its hoary peak of Sentis in the center, subdivided by the wild, and rapid torrent of the Thur which sweeps away northward through the valley of the Toggenburg, fed as it is by the fountains at Wildhaus, and the glacier on Mt. Sentis: all this forms a landscape at once bold and beautiful. This was a suitable spot for the birth-place of the great Swiss Reformer; for here nature has displayed her grandeur in unusual form. And on these Alpine heights God raised up stalwart sons, who, in after times, fought the world's battle of conscience and intellectual freedom.

WILDHAUS.

CHAPTER II.

BEGINNING LIFE.

In a plain, but substantial, dwelling located on the green meadow which stretches along the right hand side of the highway leading out of Wildhaus towards the east, as has been already intimated, we recognize the birth-place of the great Reformer. In the latter half of the fifteenth century there lived here at the border of the village of Wildhaus, surrounded by their numerous flock of children, a respectable and pious couple, Huldreich Zwingli and Margaritha, whose maiden name was Meili. Through the esteem in which this man was held by his fellow-citizens, he had been raised to the honored position of Amman, or Magistrate of the village.

This honor they had placed upon him as soon as they had obtained the authority, to elect their magistrate, their judges, and their pastor. In former years the people were not allowed this privilege. But after long continued agita-

tion, they had succeeded in wresting the right
from the Abbot of St. Gaul, who in former times
had despotic authority over all this section of
country. In its church government Wildhaus
had been under the control of Gams ; but in this
relation it had also been freed from foreign rule,
and had been raised to the position of an independent community. In the first exercise of
this privilege the people had elected Bartholomew Zwingli, the brother of the Magistrate,
their pastor. Thus we see that the Zwingli
family held a high place in the esteem of the
Wildhausers. Besides this, John Meili, a
brother of the Magistrate's wife, was the honored
abbot of Fischingen.

The family of the Magistrate consisted of
eight sons and two daughters. Ulric, the third
son, of whom we are now to hear at length, was
born on the first day of January, 1484, seven
weeks after Luther's birth-day. Though his father was the chief man of the village, little Ulric
was not to be reared in luxury. The Magistrate's house was only a plain farmer's dwelling.
Rough timbers composed its walls, and its roof
was secured by the weight of great stones laid
upon it, to keep it in place against the fury of
the winds. This house, however, was the home

of a pious couple, and here many happy hours were spent by the children, who shared in the innocent joys of a Christian household.

The parents lived in freedom and truth with one another. The wife and mother was honored not only by her ten children, but also by the villagers, and by the serving-maids and boys, who dwelt with them, and attended to the wants of the household and cultivated the meadow-land, or followed the herds and flocks, to their pasture on the Alpine heights. It was the custom then, to tell the stories of the olden times to the children during the long winter evenings; and the father would often sit, with a neighbor, at the fireside, and relate the traditions of the Toggenburg valley. This valley was associated with many events of early Swiss history; when the inhabitants had to secure themselves against the inroads of Charles the Bold, by joining the brave confederates who rolled back the enemy like avalanches from their mountain steeps.

To these stirring tales, young Ulric was one of the most eager listeners. The stories fell like living sparks of fire on his soul, and in the age of manhood they burst forth into an ardent love of home and native country.

The following poem of Schiller, will give an

idea of what these stories were like.   A brave
Knight of Toggenburg, finding that the lady of
his choice has entered a convent :

> " Springs upon his steed ;
> Summons every faithful vassal
> From his Alpine home ;
> Binds the cross upon his bosom,
> Seeks the Holy Tomb."

> There full many a deed of glory
> Wrought the hero's arm ;
> Foremost still his plumage floated,
> Where the foemen swarm ;
> Till the Moslem, terror-stricken,
> Quailed before his name ;—
> But the pang that wrings his bosom,
> Lives at heart the same.

> One long year he bears his sorrow,
> But no more can bear ;
> Rest he seeks, but finding never,
> Leaves the army there ;
> Sees a ship by Joppa's haven,
> Which, with swelling sail,
> Wafts him where his lady's breathing,
> Mingles with the gale.

> At her father's castle-portal,
> Hark ! his knock is heard :
> See ! the gloomy gate uncloses
> With the thunder word :
> " She thou seek'st is veiled forever,
> Is the bride of heaven ;
> Yester-eve the vows were plighted—
> She to God is given."

Then his old ancestral castle
   He forever flees ;
Battle-steed and trusted weapon,
   Never more he sees.
From the Toggenburg descending
   Forth unknown he glides ;
For the frame once sheathed in iron
   Now the sackcloth hides.

There beside that hallowed region,
   He hath built his bower,
Where from out the dusky lindens,
   Looked the convent-tower ;
Waiting from the morning's glimmer
   Till the day was done,
Tranquil hope in every feature,
   Sat he there alone.
*   *   *   *   *   *   *   *
If that form looked forth so lovely,
   If the sweet face smiled,
Down into the lonesome valley,
   Peaceful, angel mild.
There a corse they found him sitting,
   Once when they returned,
Still his pale and placid features,
   To the lattice turned."

At other times Ulric would listen to the accounts given by his pious Grandmother, of still earlier periods, when the godly missionaries first penetrated into the dense forests of that region of country ; men like the holy Felix and Regula, who went through the land, and taught the people the Word and cross. Then again she

2

told the stirring Bible stories, the adventures of the patriarchs, or prophets ; or told of Him who hung upon Calvary's cross that He might be a Saviour to perishing sinners. At such times the little Ulric was always an eager listener; his beaming eye and heaving breast testified that, in one heart at least, the Word of God was finding a ready response ; a response which should not be completely fulfilled until when, in after years, he should become a true minister of the Gospel of Christ.

Thus the childhood of Zwingli passed away. In this homely but cheerful dwelling was often heard the sweet strain of some musical instrument ; and there during those long winter evenings, Ulric used to try his hand at the wild Alpine melodies which to this day delight the traveler who may chance to pass through the land. These youthful efforts were the alphabet of that elaborate musical culture, which distinguished him in after years, and enabled him in part to accomplish his great work in the world, in behalf of culture and religion. But beyond this he displayed such gifts, that every one marked his wise and thoughtful spirit, which from the first distinguished him from the other children of the Magistrate's family.

From early years he was a great lover of nature. The language in which God speaks to the inhabitants of the mountain regions seemed to move his young spirit. In after years his friend Oswald Myconius wrote : " I have often thought, in my simplicity, that from these sublime heights, which stretch up towards **heaven,** he has learned something heavenly and divine."

When the spring opened, each year, the older sons and serving boys, hastened to lead the herds, and flocks, away to the mountain pastures. Usually in the first days of May, as soon as the mountains put on their coats of green, the cattle are driven up, amid the merry tinkling of bells, to the higher pastures, and ever higher and higher, a part of the inhabitants continue to ascend until, at the end of July, the loftiest heights of Sentis **are** reached. The younger children, **who are** left at home during the summer-time, to attend to the affairs of the house, and to gather the provender for the cattle during winter, sometimes hasten up the mountain steeps to celebrate with their companions, who **are** tending the flocks, merry pastoral sports, in which the joyous notes of song mix themselves with the simple tone of the Alpine horn.

As years passed on Ulric would naturally **have**

more liberty accorded to him, in which he could
observe the grandeur and beauty of the outlying
Alpine world, and begin to meditate on its mys-
teries. And thus there first awoke in his mind
the sense of the awful grandeur, and majesty, of
God,—a sentiment which in after years was destined to give him almost indomitable courage in
the great conflicts through which he was to
pass. In the solitude of the mountains, broken
only by the bells of his pasturing flocks, the re-
flective boy mused on the wisdom of God, which
reveals itself in all creatures. Inspired by these
musings doubtless he was led in after years to
compose a work on "The Providence of God."
In this work he alludes to the sagacity of the
little mice, which he had often watched in childhood days; and discourses delightfully on the
cunning little harvesters, as they make wagons
of each other, and forks, by rolling the hay
along, and using each other for hurdles in order
to carry the hay to their winter nests.

Then he rises to higher planes of thought and
says: "Do not even the things without sense
and intelligence manifest that the power, the
goodness, the renewing and sustaining energy
of God is present with them? The earth, for
example, the mother of us all, never shuts

ruthlessly her rich treasures within herself; she heeds not the wounds made on her by spade or share. The dew, the rain, the rivers, all moisten, restore, quicken within her that which had been brought to a stand still in growth by drought, and its after thriving testifies wondrously of the divine power. The mountains too, these gigan-tic, rude, inert masses, which give to the earth, as the bones to the flesh, solidity, form, and con-sistency, which render impossible or at least difficult, the passage from one place to another, which although heavier than the earth itself, yet soar far above it, and never sink ; do they not proclaim the imperishable might of Jehovah, and speak forth the whole volume of his majesty? In those works of God we behold proofs of the divine existence, and of the power, which sustains them all in being, not less than man himself."

To one thus familiar with the grandeur of Alpine scenery, from his youth, the love of that which is grand, and beautiful, must have pro-duced a lasting influence on his spirit. And he could doubtless say of his own "Sentis" what Coleridge, in his matchless "Hymn" says of Mt. Blanc:

" O dread and silent Mount! I gazed upon thee,
Till thou, still present to the bodily sense,

Didst vanish from my thought; entranced in prayer
I worshipped the Invisible alone.

Yet, like some sweet beguiling melody,
So sweet, we know not we are listening to it,
Thou, the meanwhile, wast blending with my Thought,
Yea with my Life and Life's own secret Joy:
Till the dilating soul, enrapt, transfused,
Into the mighty vision passing—there,
As in her natural form, swelled vast to Heaven!"

" Thou too, hoar Mount! with thy sky-pointing Peaks,
Oft from whose feet the Avalanche, unheard,
Shoots downward, glittering through the pure Serene
Into the depth of Clouds, that veil thy breast—
Thou too, again, stupendous Mountain! thou
That as I raise my head, awhile bowed low
In adoration, upward from thy Base
Slow travelling with dim eyes suffused with tears,
Solemnly seemest, like a vapoury cloud,
To rise before me—Rise, O ever rise,
Rise like a cloud of Incense, from the Earth!
Thou kingly Spirit throned among the hills,
Thou dread Ambassador from Earth to Heaven,
Great Hierarch! tell thou the silent Sky;
And tell the Stars, and tell yon rising Sun,
Earth with her thousand voices praises God

CHAPTER III.

THE time had now come when little Ulric was to leave the home of his childhood, and go out into the world in search of an education. The school privileges at Wildhaus seem to have been very indifferent. In many parts of the land, in those times, there were no provisions made for the regular instruction of the children; but in some places there were schools taught by men who had only a smattering of learning, who, of course, could do little more than give the mere rudiments of a primary course of instruction. In some cases older students, under the name of Lehrmeisters, traveled around, oftentimes with their wives, practising their vocations, and hiring themselves out for longer or shorter periods. An old painting, or two, still preserved in the Museum at Basel, exhibit the interior of a school-room. There the children are seen sitting, or kneeling, on the floor with their books,

23

whilst the Master, with rod in hand, is teaching a boy at the desk, while the teacher's wife is seen teaching a girl in the opposite corner.

In those schools the children and adults frequently sat on the same bench. Of course there was nothing like thorough knowledge among the masters, nothing like a division into classes, or a regular plan of instruction. Just as the natural talent of the teacher was greater or less, were the results better or worse. And yet such was the only education of a large majority of the people. Indeed thousands were destitute of even this.

Whipping was generally depended upon in order to preserve order, and to quicken the forces of intellect. The supply of whips was generally to be provided by the scholars themselves. Once each year a holiday was observed, known as the " Procession of the Rods," in which the pupils went out into the summer woods, and came back, heavily ladened with Birch-twigs, cracking jokes by the way, and singing:

" Ye fathers and ye mothers good,
    See us with the birchen-wood
    Loaded coming home again ;
    For our profit it shall serve,
    Not for injury or pain.

Your will and the command of God
Have prompted us to bear the rod
On our own bodies thus to-day,
Not in angry, sullen mood,
But with spirits glad and gay."

The course of instruction embraced, usually, three branches only : Grammar ; Music, for which the children should have been extremely grateful ; and Logic, which could not have been of any great profit to their untrained intellects. Indeed the music must have been the redeeming feature of these primitive institutions. And it was what the Swiss children loved above all else. The bright, and quick intellect of little Ulric began to manifest itself very early. His parents noticed, with pleasure, the interest he took in all matters of education. His uncle Bartholomew, who was now the minister of the church at Wesen, had also drawn the attention of his parents to his qualities which would fit him to become a student. And so when he had attained his ninth year his father, one day, set out with him for the village which was some twelve miles distant, where his uncle resided. As this was his first journey away from home it must have been fraught with great interest to the youthful traveler. One who was very

familiar with the locality thus describes the
road. "He crossed the grassy summits of the
Ammon, avoiding the wild and bold rocks which
border the lake of Wallenstadt, and arriving at
the village, entered the dwelling of the uncle,
his father's brother. "You have put lofty ideas
into Ulric's head," said the father to his brother,
"and now I have brought him, so that you may
try what he can do." "Right gladly will I
measure him," said the uncle. Then turning to
the lad he said: "So you will now be a son to
your uncle Ulric." And thus informally was
the boy installed into his new home.

When the young scholar began to look about
him, he found that his lot was cast in a beautiful
spot. Wesen as we have seen lies upon the hill-
side at the western end of the beautiful lake of
Wallenstadt, which is scarcely inferior to the
lake of Lucern in mountainous grandeur. All
along its northern side the mountains stand in
serried ranks, in places almost precipitous above
the deep blue waters. Did Ulric long to climb,
once more a mountain steep, for a holiday, he
had only to bound away up the steep sides of
the "Speer," a romantic peak rising behind the
village, and he would have a commanding pros-
pect spread out before him.

It is likely that the school which Ulric attended, in Wesen, was of the poor grade already mentioned. It is thought that the teacher only received as compensation what the scholars could beg for him in the streets, where they sang their school songs under the windows of the houses. Here the mountain boy of Wildhaus, as he may have been called, came in contact with boys who were guilty of deception and falsehood. From a child he had, what all noble natures have, a horror at the thought of lying. He once said in after years : " Lying ought to be more severely punished than theft. Hypocrisy is worse than stealing. Falsehood is the beginning of all evil. Man most resembles God by being true. Glorious is the truth, full of majesty, commanding the respect of the wicked."

His uncle soon perceived that the Wesen school could do nothing more for Ulric. The scholar was already too far advanced for his teacher; some more advanced school must be found for him. After consultation with his parents, it was resolved to send him away to Basel. It was a great way from home to be sure ; an hundred miles at least ; and only slow methods of travel were known in that day.

Basel and Geneva are the gateways to Swit-

zerland. The one stands at the north-west
angle, where the majestic Rhine issues forth
from the glacier-fed springs and clear blue lakes,
which ever supply his mighty current. The
other stands on the less majestic Rhone, which
opens a gateway through the mountains to
France and the Mediterranean Sea.

To this day Basel is noted for its schools;
even for its schools of theology. But when
Ulric arrived there, the fame of the city, in this
respect, was already well established, for its
University, founded in 1464, was then resorted
to from all parts of the west, by the youth
who sought a liberal education. Besides this,
Basel was noted for its publishing interests,
which, at that time, were just beginning to be
appreciated at something like their true value;
the printing-press had then only been lately
invented, and all learned men understood what
a great advantage would result from having the
printed texts of classical, and other works, used
in the higher instruction given at the universities.

And then there were a number of learned
men, like the Wessels, and Wittenbachs, and
above all, Erasmus of Rotterdam, who were
engaged in giving instruction, in the higher

grades of learning, at Basel. However, the mounta'n-boy of Wildhaus is yet too young to avail himself of these advanced teachers; and so he is sent to the Theodore school, an institution presided over by Gregory Binzli, an excellent, not unlearned man, of a very amiable disposition. He took a great liking to Zwingli, who soon stood in the foremost rank among his school fellows, a master in debate, and the possessor of an extraordinary talent for music. Learned discussions, much in vogue in that day, among the doctors of universities, had descended even to the children of the schools. Ulric took part in them, and in contest with the pupils of other schools, frequently bore off the prize. His signal success in these efforts, it is said, aroused the jealousy of his seniors; and his teacher, perceiving that his school was not adapted to the capacities of his pupil any longer, after three years, sent him home, with the advice that he should be sent to a more advanced school.

Ulric was now about 13 years of age. He was bright and vivacious, and his musical talents began to develop themselves in an extraordinary degree, and to excite universal admiration. It could not be expected that his parents would now arrest him in his course of study; and give him charge once more of their herds and flocks at Wildhaus.   A conference was held between them and his uncle Bartholomew, as before, the result of which was that the lad was sent to school at a city nearly as far distant from home as Basel was.

Preparations began at once to be made, and not many days had passed ere the mountain-boy was on his way towards the city of Bern, whither his parents had now resolved to send him.

The city of Bern is said to have been founded in the year 1191, by Berthold Vth, who gave it the name " Bären," in German signifying a bear, because he had killed a bear on the spot. It is situated on the banks of the Aare, which, in the winding course it follows at this point, encompasses the promontory on which the city stands, on three sides.   The modern city has an imposing appearance from a distance, and a nearer view discloses one of the best and most regularly built towns in Europe, as it is the finest in Switzerland.

At almost every point the traveller sees something at Bern to remind him of the origi-nal bruin, which was slain here so many years ago. At one point he will suddenly come upon two granite columns, formed by the sculptor to represent gigantic bears in the act of rearing, and ready to seize their prey. In another place bruin is seen, equipped with shield, sword, banner, and helmet. A whole troop of bears go through a performance on the dial of the town-clock, two minutes before every hour. Images of bears are for sale at all the market stalls; and a stranger is apt to think that Bruin must be the patron saint of the city.

The people of Bern seem to have been a merry race from the beginning. The scenery surrounding it is delightful; the windings of the Aare give it picturesqueness, and a wild beauty, and in the distance one may see the ever majestic Alps.

When young Zwingli came hither he entered the school of Henry Lupulus. His teacher was noted for his correct knowledge of the ancient Classics, and he soon infused a spirit of research and study in this direction, on the part of his pupil, Ulric, who was only too well pleased to pursue the studies marked out for him by his teacher. He was very proficient here, as he had been at Basel. The teacher had made a pilgrimage to Jerusalem, and was accustomed to speak of Palestine to his pupils, as of a land of peculiar interest, because of its sacred associations. Under Lupulus Ulric acquired a flowing style in writing and speaking. He became a good scholar, not in the corrupt monks' Latin, but learned the highly cultivated, clear, powerful language, which had come down from classical times. He learned to speak Latin, he afterward said, better than he spoke his native tongue. He also became familiar with the history of the most celebrated Republic of antiquity, which, to the Swiss, themselves the citizens of a free country, was full of interest.

Ulric also zealously applied himself to music; and learned to play on all the instruments then known, including the lute, with which he accompanied his singing. This attracted the attention of the Dominican friars, who were anxious to have him enter their order, that they might profit by his musical talents, and thus offset their rivals, the Franciscans. But the eye of God watched over the lad, and preserved him from the snares of these corrupted monks. His father and uncle heard of the danger which impended over him, and they recalled him home, to send him elsewhere. He was now prepared for the high school, and they accordingly decided to send him to Vienna, where a celebrated school was established.

At this school the mountain-boy formed the acquaintance of two Swiss students, Joachim Von Watt, called Vadian, and Henry Loreti, who was sometimes called Glareanus, because he came from Glarus. The three Swiss youths, united in the bonds of close friendship, devoted themselves, with great success, to the investigation of the sciences, and also continued the study of the classics.

Ulric remained here for two years, laying in rich stores of learning; when he was called home by his father about the year 1502. The desire to prosecute his studies, and also to apply the results of his industry, led him shortly afterwards to proceed to Basel once more. There he became a teacher in the school of St. Martin, and taught Latin with great success. Soon after this he placed himself under the instruction of the learned Thomas Wittenbach. His fellow-student, and intimate friend here, was one Leo Juda. The two young men devoted themselves to the study of the higher branches of learning with unwearied assiduity. Their eminent teacher was not only well versed in the ancient languages, but he added to this a profound ac-

3

quaintance with the Holy Scriptures. Out of
the barren deserts of school-wisdom, destitute
of all water, it was this excellent man's habit to
lead his pupils to the living sources of God's
word, and teach them to draw water from thence
for themselves, and their flocks. "The time is
not far distant," said Wittenbach, "when the
scholastic theology will be swept away, and the
old doctrine of the church established in its
room, on the foundation of the Bible. Absolution is a Romish cheat; the death of Christ is
the only payment for our sins." Such a seed-
corn as this, found in the heart of Zwingli, so
receptive of the true, a soil in which its roots
struck vigorously, shot up strongly, and bore
noble fruit at an after day.

After hard study, the recreation of the two
friends was vocal and instrumental music.
Leo poured forth a fine treble, while Zwingli
accompanied him on any one of the instruments,
of which he was the acknowledged master.
Thus were the graver labors of study relieved
with a recreation at once useful and delightful,
which afterwards did them good service in the
pastorate.

Soon after this Zwingli was honored with the
degree, "Master of Arts," which he accepted,

more out of deference to the prejudices of men, who weigh the learning by the title, than from any sense of its intrinsic worth. He at no time made use of the degree, being wont to say, "One is our Master, even Christ."

But while he cared little for the titles that men honor, as expressive of high attainments, he honored learning itself. He was enthusiastic in his studies of the classics; delighted in the poems of Hesiod, Homer, and Pindar, on the latter two preparing notes in the way of a commentary. He studied closely Cicero and Demosthenes, that he might learn of oratory and politics; and he also loved the wonders of nature as reported by Pliny, Thucydides, Sallust. Livy, Cæsar, Suetonius, Plutarch, and Tacitus, were all familiar to him. He has been blamed for his devotion to these great authors; as he thought that he discerned in them not mere human virtues, but the influence of the Holy Spirit. God's dealings, he thought, in olden times were not limited to the Holy Land, but extended to all the earth. "Plato, also," said he, "drew from a source divine; and if the Catos, Camillus, and Scipios, had not been deeply religious, could they have acted so nobly as we know they did?" However, when the Word of God was afterward opened to him in all its fullness, these early student views were greatly modified, and then he could truly say: " One is our Master, even Christ." And here ends the story of Zwingli's student life. He was always a student; he never relaxed his efforts for an extended culture. And no fact is more surely established than that Zwingli was not only one of the best scholars of his time ; but also that he excelled in love of justice and truth.

CHAPTER IV.

THE YOUNG PRIEST OF GLARUS.

IT is sometimes difficult for us to realize that, 400 years ago, there was no Protestant church in existence, and that there were but few persons then living, who thought that the church could be reformed. Since the days of Constantine the Great, who was Emperor of Rome and of all the east, and who came to the height of his power, at the time when the Council of Nice was held, A. D. 325; and declared that Christianity was the religion of the State, the church of Rome had held almost complete sway over the various nations of Western Europe. The north-Rhine peoples who overran the Italian States in the fifth and sixth centuries, were themselves captured by the religion of their captives, and embraced the Christian faith, acknowledging the Pope of Rome as their supreme Pontiff, and vieing with each other in their readiness to carry out his behests. For centuries this con-

37

dition of things lasted, until now, in the fifteenth century, when Luther and Zwingli were born, no other form of Christianity was ever thought of, beside that which looked to the Pope, as the Vicar of Christ on earth, and obediently placed the neck under his heavy yoke.

The church, through its great prosperity, and almost universal sway, had become very corrupt. The Pope, it was thought, had power to pardon sins. The ministers were all called priests, and it was their chief duty to exhort the people to be loyal to the Pope, and the Cardinals, and other dignitaries; and to come regularly to the confessional, and acknowledge to the priest what sins they were guilty of, when he would pronounce their full pardon. The priests were not allowed to marry; and on this account great abuses had crept into the church; and it was well known that there was great impurity prevailing among the monks and nuns, who lived in the convents and monasteries. It is true that pure-minded persons like John Huss, in Bohemia, and Savonorola in Italy, and Wyclifle in England, and others had arisen from time to time, and testified against the abuses existing in the church; but they were only told to recant, and when they refused to do this, they were put to death. And so the reign of the Pope had become a reign of terror; and though the Popes were often very evil men, yet they were to be obeyed, even at the perils of suffering a martyr's death.

Zwingli became a priest in the Romish church. The reader will not be surprised at this, when he remembers that this was the only course open, at that time, to any one who sought the office of the ministry. When there was but one outward organization, to which all the ministers and the people were obedient, the candidate for the ministry must seek permission to preach, through its authority. Zwingli was ordained to the priesthood, by the Bishop of Constance in 1506, one year previous to the ordination of Luther at Erfurth, in Saxony.

During this year Zwingli received a call to be the pastor of the church at Glarus. He accepted the call, and at once made preparations to enter upon his charge. His invitation was the more acceptable because he was elected by the free votes of the community. He was encouraged with the thought that he had well improved the season of preparation. God had preserved him against gross declensions, despite the general wickedness and corruptions of the time. "I acknowledge myself," are his words, "to be a great sinner before God, but I have not lived immorally, and on no occasion has discipline been exercised upon me." With a heart overflowing with gratitude for the divine direction, he exclaimed, " God has granted me, from the age of boyhood, to devote myself to the acquirement of knowledge, human and divine." And he resolved again to be true and upright in every situation in life in which the hand of the Lord might yet place him.

It was near the close of the year 1506, when the young priest, who had now reached his twenty-second year, set out from his childhood home at Wildhaus where he had been spending a short time with his parents, for his new charge at Glarus. He had gone over once more the haunts of his childhood plays. He had looked up to the heights of Sentis and recalled the solemn thoughts of his early years, when he used to think that the very mountains reflected the presence and power of Jehovah. And on the preceding Sabbath he had said his first " Mass " in the little church at Wildhaus, in the presence of his father's family, thus formally announcing to his old friends his determination to give himself to the work of the ministry for life.

The solemn service concluded, the young Parson bade farewell to his father's household, and set out again from Wildhaus, and crossed the Ammon to Wesen, as he had done thirteen years before. How different life appeared to him now that he had mingled with the world, and penetrated the mystery that ever enshrouds the cloister and the academy to the aspiring youth! Instead of being the untutored mountain-boy who visited his uncle Bartholomew, on the former occasion, he now comes to him as one who has passed honorably through the ordeal of hard study, and is admitted to equal honors with himself.

Wesen was the market town of the people who dwelt at Glarus. It was only seven and a half miles distant, in a southerly direction, and thus only some twenty miles from Wildhaus. Having preached at Rapperschwyl, a town situated on the lake of Zurich, he went on towards Glarus. From Wesen he pursued his way along the banks of the Linth, by a path which here winds between high and rocky mountains, to his place of destination, which was the chief town of the canton.

Before Zwingli could enter on his sacred office, he was destined to have a painful experience of the system of corruption under which his country groaned. One Henry Goeldli, the descendant of an aristocratic house, who was at that time "Master of the Horse" to the Pope, and a boon companion of his holiness, appeared with a papal letter of investiture for the place, although he was already in the possession of several livings. The community of Glarus maintained their right of election with success; yet Zwingli was obliged to indemnify the papal intruder with a sum of money, for renouncing claims that were totally groundless.

Zwingli now devoted himself to his chosen pursuit. His charge was situated in a beautiful, though narrow, valley. All around were the lofty summits of the Alps. The village lay at the north-east base of the precipitous and imposing "Vorder-Glarnisch" over seven thousand six hundred feet in height; and at the south-east of the "Wiggis," the barren grey summits of which formed a striking contrast to the fresh green of the valley. The "Haustock," ten thousand feet in height, formed the back-ground to the south, and at the west was the "Schild," over seven thousand five hundred feet in height. Thus as the mountains were round about Jerusalem, so were there mountains, and much higher ones, around Glarus. The people at Glarus were hardy mountaineers. Some of them dwelt on the mountain side, and mined the slate and prepared it for market. Others dwelt in the narrow valley and prepared the celebrated Swiss cheese so highly prized in many places to this day. Among these people Zwingli was now to labor. He was profoundly sensible that the servant of God, in the care of souls, must apply himself unremittingly to serious study, if he would guard his soul against the inroads of a low worldliness, and if he would proclaim the truth to his hearers, with living conviction.

What idea Zwingli entertained of the pastoral office, appears from the course he marked out for himself, and steadily pursued. "He becomes a priest," writes his friend Myconius," and contrary to the usual way of priests, he yields himself to his studies, especially to that of theology. Now he first rightly apprehends how much he, who is intrusted with the instruction of the people in divine truth, ought himself, before all things, to be furnished with theological knowledge, and then to possess eloquence also, that he may be enabled to exhibit everything both truly and profitably, agreeably to the capacities of his

hearers. To these studies he applied himself
with a diligence of which there had been no previous example in many years."

The diligence of Zwingli must have been remarkable, for beside the care of the church in
the village, he had three other congregations,
comprising nearly a third part of the canton.
Yet with all his other duties he was unremitting
in his devotion to his studies. The Roman
classics he continued to read with diligence,
chiefly that they might be useful to him in his
acquisition of truth, and in the cultivation of his
oratorical powers. "As for truth itself, he went
for it," says Myconius, "and drew it, with
untiring industry, out of the perennial stream
of God's word. Although he knew Holy Scripture, as yet only in the Latin version, he passed
among his fellow priests for one who had a profound knowledge of the Bible. He well knew,
however, and deeply felt, how small was the
title he had to such a distinction. He was
ambitious to excel in public speaking, and to
this end he persevered in his study of the Latin.
The great orators of antiquity, those masters of
eloquence, whom he regarded as unrivalled,
were ever present to him, and the desire burned
within him to work, with the power of oratory,

in Switzerland, and in the cause of divine truth, yet greater wonders than these had ever wrought by their eloquence in Italy.

He now labored to establish a Latin school in Glarus, and to befriend many poor students who began, or continued their education there. He soon gathered around him a noble band of young men, whom he led on to the pursuit of an education, and to a high standing in the community, who might otherwise have missed their opportunity for improvement altogether. Among his scholars was his younger brother James, whose education he superintended with brotherly affection. As soon as the students were prepared for the high school he sent them away either to the high school at Vienna, where the friend of his youth Vadian had risen to the rank of professor and rector; or to Basel where Glarean, also his friend, taught the high school, the excellent man boarding the students himself, that he might the better watch over their education and morals.

But wherever his students went, they bore, engraved on their hearts, the memory of their first master, and maintained with him a correspondence of which the following is a specimen. Peter Tschudi wrote him from Paris: "Thou

art to us like a guardian angel ;" and his brother
wrote from another place : " Help, help me, that
I may be recalled to thee, for nowhere do I like
so well to dwell as near thyself." Their cousin,
Valentine Tschudi, and Zwingli's successor at
Glarus, wrote : " Can I ever cease to be grateful
to thee for thy great benefits ?" " On every
occasion that I return to my home, and lately
in an especial manner, when I was four days
suffering under fever, and again, when I left my
books behind me in Basel, and when in my
timidity I feared to be burdensome to thee, thou
gavest me thy books, thy help, thy services.
Ah ! the whole benevolence of thy soul over-
flowed to me, and it was not in any general way
that the rich treasures of thy learning were
placed at my disposal, but with a special regard
to my peculiar circumstances and necessities."
Testimonies like these bear witness to the great
kindness of heart which characterized the young
pastor at Glarus. While evidences are also at
hand to prove his undoubted abilities. The
learned Erasmus wrote to him from Basel : "All
hail ! say I, to the Swiss people, whom I have
always admired, whose intellectual and moral
qualities yourself, and men such as yourself, are
training."

Doubtless this opinion of Erasmus was formed during the visit which Zwingli made to Basel in 1514. All the men of learning assembled round the scholar from Rotterdam, who seems at once to have selected Zwingli as the man who promised to be the glory of Switzerland. This visit had a great influence upon the youthful pastor of Glarus ; for here he met Myconius, and John Hausschein, afterwards called Oecolampadius, who was pastor of Basel, and a man of great learning also, and in sympathy with the reformatory views, held by the few advanced minds in the little coterie. It was at this time that Erasmus said: "We must seek but one thing in Holy Scriptures, namely, Jesus Christ." Zwingli returned to his mountain home, greatly strengthened by this conference, and filled with new views of the important duties of his pastorate.

With reference to the feelings with which he discharged these duties, he afterward wrote: "Young as I was, the office of the priesthood filled me with greater fear than joy, for this was ever present to me, that the blood of the sheep who perished through any neglect or guilt of mine, would be required at my hands."

CHAPTER V.

WARS AND RUMORS OF WARS.

WE are now to be introduced to other scenes in the life of Zwingli, quite different from those we have hitherto considered. It might be inferred that the life of the young priest at Glarus would be uneventful, being confined chiefly to those cares that commonly mark the experience of the country curate. Such however was not to be the case with Zwingli. Though he was a student from choice and inclination, yet the times in which he lived, and the interests of his country, called him forth from his limited sphere of operations in Glarus to participate in the stirring events of war.

The remote cause of this remarkable change in the life of the young pastor, was the influence of a noted dignitary of the Romish church named Cardinal Schinner. He was a man of extraordinary powers, who had raised himself

48

from the condition of herd-boy, to be Bishop Prince of the land, and a Cardinal of the Church. It is related that when he was a poor boy, attending the school at Sion, in the Valais, he was one day singing in the streets, for his bread, when an old man called him to him, and said: "Thou shalt become a bishop and a prince." The boy was filled with a burning ambition from that hour, and determined to fulfill the prophecy, if possible. He attended school at Zurich and Como, and thus became proficient both in German and Italian; and after ordination to the priesthood, rose rapidly in the estimation of churchmen, and soon attained distinction.

Rumor had it that he was sent to Rome to obtain a bishopric for one who had been selected for that office; but with a tricky heart, he asked the appointment for himself, and the Pope granted it, so that the messenger went home as the bishop of Sion. A man who could perform an act like this was sure to be engaged in unholy schemes thereafter; and when Louis XII, of France, was at war with the Popes Julius II, and Leo X, Schinner knew that each party would be glad to retain the Swiss in his service. Accordingly he offered his services to Louis, and named his price. The king remarked: "It

4

is too much for any one man." "I will show
him," replied the bishop of Sion, in a passion,
"that I am a man worth purchasing at any
cost." From that time he engaged to act with
the Pope Julius II, who received his advances
with joy.

By the year 1510, Schinner had succeeded,
by his arts, in attaching the Swiss to the interests of the papacy; so that these hardy mountaineers, for absolution, some deceitful promises,
and but a scanty pay, lent themselves as tools
to forward the ambitious plans of the Popes.
There was scarcely a man of weight in the
country, whom this man had not gained over to
the papacy, by the glittering bait of some post
of honor, or other favor.

The noble form of the talented pastor of Glarus, standing high in the esteem of his people,
caught the eye of the artful bishop. Zwingli
on account of his poverty, had not been able to
purchase books sufficient to meet the demands
of his thirst for knowledge; here was a capital
opportunity to take him in the papal toils.
Schinner hastened to inform him that the Pope
had set apart an annual sum of fifty florins, in
order that he might freely pursue his studies.
In return, Zwingli's talents and energies were

to be devoted to the Pope. Had he acceded to this condition, the mountain boy of Wildhaus might well have climbed the ladder of papal promotion as high as the herd-boy of Wallis, the bishop prince and Cardinal, had done.

Zwingli has this to say regarding his acceptance of this offer: "I confess here, before God and all the world, my sin" (in drawing the above annual sum, which he did accept, and use conditionally): "for before the year 1516, I hung mightily on the Roman power, and thought it highly becoming in me to take the money, although I told the Romish ambassadors in clear and express terms, when they exhorted me to preach nothing against the Pope, they were not to fancy that I, for their money, should withhold one iota of the truth, so they might take back, or give it, as they pleased." The Popes and the Cardinal had more at heart the success of their policy than the victory of the truth, and so they left Zwingli alone for the present, with the little stipend which he expended in the purchase of books at Basel.

In the meantime Cardinal Schinner and the Pope threw off all disguise; and began to recruit soldiers in Switzerland for the campaign against the King of France, who was making

inroads on the papal territory in Italy. Eight
thousand Swiss were persuaded by the Cardinal
to enlist for the campaign. They crossed the
Alps, and were marshalled with the papal
army; but receiving scant pay, and being
worsted by the French, they retreated in-
gloriously to their own mountain home. They
brought with them evil and dissipated habits,
which resulted in licentiousness, violence and
general disorder. The citizens arose against
their magistrates, the children against their
parents, the lands were allowed to go uncultiva-
ted, and the shepherds neglected their herds
and flocks. Luxury and beggary increased, the
most sacred ties were severed, and the confederacy seemed in danger of dissolution.

Zwingli could not help noticing the peril. In
order to counteract the evil influences resulting
from mercenary warfare he wrote and published
a poem entitled "The Labyrinth;" and another
entitled: "A Poetic Fable concerning an Ox
and several Beasts." He described the mazes
of a mysterious garden, where Minos had concealed the Minotaur, a monster half man and
half bull, whom he feeds with the blood of the
Athenian youth. He interpreted the Minotaur
as the sin, the irreligion, and the foreign service
of the Swiss which devour their children.

A brave man, Theseus, undertakes to deliver his country. He meets, first, a lion with one eye; it is Spain and Arragon. Next he meets a crowned eagle, with open throat; it is the Empire; then he encounters a cock with crest erect; it is France. But the hero overcomes them all; and at last delivers his country. Had the warning been heeded, it would have been well for the Swiss, but so great was the infatuation that the protest was unheeded, and great loss was the consequence.

Another campaign was undertaken by Schinner in the early part of 1513, to cross the Alps and drive the French out of Lombardy. As the banner of Glarus was unfurled in this expedition, Zwingli was appointed, by an order of the magistracy, and in conformity with an old Swiss custom, to follow the army as a field preacher. At one sweep Lombardy was cleared of the invaders, and the Duke Maximilian Sforza reinstated in his hereditary dominions, the duchy of Milan. After the fortunate issue of this campaign, a papal embassy, presented by the hands of Zwingli, the proud victors in the war, with a richly gilt sword and a ducal hat, emblazoned with pearls and gold, over which the Holy Spirit hovered, in the form of a dove. At the

same time, the honorary title was bestowed
upon them of "Deliverers of the Church!"
The present was very welcome to the victorious
Confederates, as well as the words which accompanied it: "They may ask what they will, the
holiest shall not be denied them." The greater
part begged that they might be permitted to
carry the image of the crucified Redeemer on
their banners: the men of Glarus desired to
carry that of the risen Saviour.

A second time, in 1515, the Swiss army once
more crossed the Alps to fight against the
French army, and Zwingli as before, accompanied them as field preacher. On this occasion it was the policy of the French monarch to
cast the seeds of disunion in the Swiss ranks,
by bribing some of the leaders. He succeeded
in dividing the Swiss host, and in inducing a
part of it, by a treaty the terms of which were
in the highest degree disgraceful to the Swiss,
to return home. Zwingli, who penetrated the
false game that was playing, and perceived the
mischief that brooded over his country, raised
his voice loudly against the treaty, in a sermon
which he preached to the army, in the square
at Monza, on the 7th of September. He exhorted the assembled warriors to be true to

each other—to union and watchfulness in the presence of their dangerous foe. " Had they followed him," said his friend Steiner, who shared the dangers of the campaign with him, " much mischief would have been prevented." But the warning of their chaplain was unheeded; the treaty was signed, according to the terms of which, a part of the Swiss withdrew.

A short time afterward the remnant of the army under the fiery exhortations of Cardinal Schinner, imprudently joined in a skirmish with the French. In this skirmish the battle of Marignano took its origin, in which the Swiss, on the first day, maintained the field with a tremendous loss; but on the second day, being attacked by the French with fresh forces, they were beaten after a desperate stand, and forced to retreat on Milan. Zwingli himself, according to the reports of eye witnesses, displayed striking proofs of personal courage, both by word and deed. His intrepid but serious behavior, as well as his sermons, breathing at once zeal in behalf of the truth, and love for his native country, won for him the hearts of all the better confederates.

It has been regretted by many that Zwingli was led to accompany the Swiss army into Italy.

It is indeed to be regretted that war has not yet ceased from the earth. But the causes of the war in Zwingli's time lay far beyond his reach and influence, and the only question left for him to decide, was whether he would conform to the ancient custom of his country, and go with the soldiers from his own charge as their chaplain, or whether he would remain at home and continue his denunciations against the evils of a war engaged in with a mercenary spirit.

It was represented to him also that this war was undertaken to reclaim the ancient possessions of the church in which he was a minister. Lombardy had been the home of the church for centuries, and the foe who threatened her was a civil power, which simply sought its own advantage without reference to the question of principle. France was no friend to the Swiss; and as long as the church of Rome was the accepted church of Switzerland, so long would there be a foundation for her to call upon the Swiss for aid.

To blame Zwingli for accepting the chaplaincy, at this time, and also subsequently, when he went with the troops from Zurich to the field of Cappel, would be like condemning the ministers

who acted as chaplains in our own late civil war.
War can only be justified when it is a necessity.
And when engaged in it should be from good
motives, either in self-defence, or to protect the
weak and helpless. Zwingli preached a great
deal on the subject, both before and after these
campaigns, and in all his utterances he clearly
distinguishes between the mercenary spirit of the
soldier who is a hireling merely, and that of the
patriot who fights in defence of his native land.

This is well set forth in the poem alluded to
above, in which he represents the confederacy,
under the symbol of an ox, which was led astray
by artful cats, though warned by faithful dogs,
and by that means lost his liberty.

> " Where bribery can show its face,
> There Freedom has no dwelling-place.
> Freedom must stand by Bravery,
> Sheltered and guarded evermore.
> Amid the bloody ranks of war,
> Amid the fearful dance of death,
> Let gleaming swords drawn from the sheath,
> And sharp-edged spears and axes be,
> Thy guardians golden Liberty.
> But, where a brutish heart is met,
> And by a tempting bribe beset,
> There noble Freedom, glorious boon !
> And name and blood of friends too soon,
> Are cheaply prized ; and rudely torn
> The oaths in holy covenant sworn."

CHAPTER VI.

FOES NEARER HOME.

ONE advantage, at least, came to Zwingli from his visit to Italy. While at Milan he found time, after having attended to the wounded soldiers, to visit the library, and while there he came upon an old " Mass-book," used in the time of St. Ambrose. It differed materially from the one that was then put into the hands of all the priests by the church, to be invariably used by them in the conduct of public worship. This led him to the following train of reasoning : " Either Bishop Ambrose, from whom the mass-book emanated, has made changes in the existing one, without his being visited with censure, or the Romish ritual has taken its present shape since his time. In either case, it is evident that the liturgy of the mass is the work of man, and subject to change. The Word of God alone is eternal and unchangeable."

One day Zwingli happened to be in the parsonage of his friend parson Adam at Mollis, in company also with the pastor of Wesen, and his former teacher at Basel, George Binzli. Zwingli found another liturgy, two hundred years old, in which a sentence occurred which showed that at that time, both the bread and the cup had been given to the laity, though that custom was now discontinued. He called attention to this fact, and commented upon it. The inquiring, and investigating spirit of Zwingli led him to examine into the authority of the church for himself; he had always been an independent thinker.

In the year 1513 he began the study of the Greek language, in order that he might be able to read the New Testament in the original. He acquired the language without any assistance, and in a short time. He extended his reading, in the Greek, to the writings of the Fathers, that he might learn their comments on the Bible. He said that he read the Fathers, "as one asks a friend what he means." And Myconius adds : " He perceived however that the Holy Spirit alone can give the true meaning of the Word which he himself has indited; and he looked up to heaven, for direction, wrestled with God in prayer, that he would bestow upon him the inestimable blessing of his Holy Spirit, and it was granted to him, ever more and more, to pierce into the sense of the Word."

The Word of God now became his daily companion. In his studies he compared one passage with another, and interpreted the darker by the plainer, so that it was apparent to every one that heard him commenting on a difficult passage, that not man, but the Spirit himself was his teacher. We cannot help admiring the zeal of Zwingli in the study of the Scriptures, especially when he devoted himself to the study of the Greek, without assistance, and with only the poor lexicons and grammars of that day, in order that he might understand the teachings of the New Testament. Such was his devotion, that he wrote in 1513 : "Nothing can again withdraw me from the study of the Greek."

One circumstance particularly, shows how zealous he was in his studies. He copied, with his own hand, in Greek characters, all the Epistles of St. Paul, that he might carry them about with him, and be able to consult them at all times. The manuscript was presented to the library of Zurich in 1563, by Anna Zwingli, the last of the Reformer's descendants. It consisted of forty-three sheets, in pocket form, with large margins which are filled with notes in a very small hand, and was designed evidently for a pocket edition.

Zwingli's spiritual life was greatly quickened at this time also. He read a poem of Erasmus his learned friend, whom he had met at Basel, in which the Saviour is represented as complaining that men do not seek all good from him, who is the source of all good, the Comforter, the Guardian of the soul. He then thought, he says: "Why do we seek help of the creature?" His sermons now became more impassioned and earnest. Myconius says that he: "Now began, after the example of Christ, to denounce, from the pulpit, certain base vices, which were extremely prevalent, especially the taking of gifts from princes, and baleful mercenary wars; for he saw clearly that the doctrine of divine truth would never find an entrance until these sources of iniquity were closed. He proclaimed evangelical truth, without making any allusion to Romish errors, or with a very slight reference to them. He wished truth first to make its way to the hearts of his hearers, for, thought he, if the true be once comprehended, the false will be easily detected as such."

But these utterances, as might be supposed,

stirred up a tide of opposition against the young pastor. The custom of enlisting as soldiers for pay still went on, and the plain rebukes, though greatly deserved, were very unwelcome. Enemies began to circulate reports adverse to his character. They said that he had received pecuniary rewards himself; no doubt in reference to the little stipend, formerly accepted by him, for the purchase of books. They tried to fasten upon him the charge of frivolity; no doubt citing his fondness for music, which taste never deserted him. When weary with the work of the pastorate, or of his profound studies, he would again resort to the recreation of his student life. Taking up the lute, harp, violin, flute, dulcimer, or hunting-horn, he would pour forth gladsome sounds, as in days of old at Wildhaus, or when at school at Basel, when he used to make his room, or the apartment of some friend, ring again with the airs of his beloved country, accompanying them with his own songs.

Whatever may have been the precise form which the opposition took, the animating impulse was an unworthy one, and yet it made the burden of the pastorate heavy to be borne. At last the opposition took the form of a charge of heresy. Notwithstanding his wise moderation

in general, he had laid himself, in some measure,
liable by agitating the cause of reform, both in
matters pertaining to the church and state. In
this he had only done that which was his bounden
duty, nevertheless it furnished the pretext
desired by his opponents.

These foes nearer home, than were the Cardinals or the French, will at last see the bold
and learned minister, departing to a new field
of labor. But before we follow him to his second charge, it will be well for us to ask whether
Zwingli was an independent Reformer at this
time, or was a mere imitator of other men; (e. g.
of Luther,) who labored in other parts of Germany and Switzerland. That he had laid the
foundation for (his work while in Glarus cannot
be doubted. His discovery that the church fathers did not agree among themselves ; that the
form of the Mass had been changed; and that the
Scriptures alone are the sure rule of faith and
practice, were the entering wedges that would
lead him very soon to break away from the traditions and the abuses existing in the church.

It was about the year 1516, that Zwingli
arrived at the views here presented, which he
afterwards reduced to writing as follows : "We
see, thought I, the whole of mankind striving,

their lives long, after the attainment of future bliss, not perhaps directed to this pursuit so much from any natural impulse as from the instinct of self-preservation implanted in us by the Author of our being at our creation; yet the opinions are very various as to how this great end is to be obtained. If we go to the philosophers, we find them disputing on this subject in a manner which makes us turn away from them with a feeling of disgust. If we seek for a solution of the problem from the Christians, we find here even a greater diversity of opinion than prevails among the heathen, for some are striving to reach the goal in the way of human tradition, and by the elements of this world (Col. 2 : 8) *i. e.*, by their own and human opinions, while others are relying entirely on God's grace and promises : both the one and the other, however, are equally urgent that those who come to them for consolation, should adopt their sentiments.

While I was reflecting on this diversity of opinion in the earthen vessels, and praying to God that He would show me an outlet to the state of uncertainty it produces, He says, "Fool, dost thou not remember the Word of the Lord abideth forever?" Hold to this. And again,

" Heaven and earth shall pass away, but My word shall not pass away." What is human perishes ; what is divine, is unchangeable. And, " in vain they honor Me, teaching for doctrines the commandments of men." For this cause I put every thing aside, and came to the point, that I would rely on no single thing, on no single word, so firmly as on that which comes from the mouth of the Lord.

I now began to weigh with myself, whether there were no means by which one might recognize what was human and what divine. Then the passsage occurred to me, all is clear in the light, in that light, to wit, which says : " I am the Light of the World, that lightens every man that cometh into the world ;" and again, " believe every spirit, but try the spirits, whether they be of God." Seeking for the touchstone of truth, I find none other but that stone of stumbling and the rock of offence to all who, after the manner of the Pharisees, set their own commandments in the place of God's. I now began to test every doctrine by this test. Did I see that the touchstone gave back the same color, or rather, that the doctrine could bear the brightness of the stone, I accepted it ; if not, I cast it away. And if any one brought

5

forward any other doctrine or threats, I said:
"we ought to obey God rather than men." From
this time his watch-word was: "The Word of
God the only reliable rule of Faith and Life;
and Christ our only Salvation."

Surely this was good Protestant doctrine;
and in attaining it Zwingli did not consult with
flesh and blood, but with the Word of truth.
Afterward his enemies said that he had bor-
rowed from Luther. And to this he felt con-
strained to make the following reply: "I began
to preach the Gospel before a single individual
in our part of the country ever heard the name
of Luther. This was in 1516. Who called me
a Lutheran then? When Luther's exposition of
the Lord's Prayer appeared, it so happened that
I had shortly before preached from Matthew
on the same Prayer. Well, some good folks,
who everywhere found my thoughts in Luther's
work, would hardly let themselves be made to
believe that I had not written this book myself;
they fancied that, being afraid to put my name
to it, I had set that of Luther instead.

Who then called me a follower of Luther?
Then, how comes it that the Romish Cardinals
and Legates, who were at that very time at Zurich, never reproached me as Lutheran, until

they had·declared Luther a heretic, which, however, they could never make him? When they
had branded him a heretic, it was then for the
first time they exclaimed, I was Lutheran;
although Luther's name was entirely unknown to
me during these two years that I kept to the
Bible alone. But it is part of their cunning policy
to load me and others with this name. Do they
say: "you must be Lutheran for you preach as
Luther;" I answer, I preach too as Paul writes,
why not call me a Pauline? nay; I preach the
Word of Christ, why not much rather call me a
Christian? In my opinion, Luther is one of God's
chosen heralds and combatants, who searches the
Scriptures with greater zeal than has been done
by any man on earth for the last thousand years.

"Therefore, dear Christians, let not the name
of Christ be changed into the name of Luther, for
Luther has not died for us, but he teaches us to
know Him from whom alone our salvation comes.
If Luther preaches Christ, he does it as I do;
although, God be praised for it, an innumerable
multitude, much more than by me, and by
others, have been converted to God through
him, for God metes out to every man as He will.
For my part, I shall bear no other name but
that of my Captain, Jesus Christ, whose soldier

I am. No man can esteem Luther higher than
I do. Yet I testify before God and all men, that
I never, at any time, wrote to him, or he to me,
nor has anything been done to open up a correspondence, between us. I have purposely abstain-
ed from all correspondence with him, not that I
feared any man on this account, but because I
would have it appear how uniform the Spirit of
God is, in so far that we, who are far distant from
each other, and have held no communication, are
yet of the same mind, and this without the
slightest concert. But I will not be so bold as to
place myself by the side of Luther, for each of us
works according to the ability given us of God."

The candor and modesty of this language is
worthy of the greatest admiration. Particularly
is this noteworthy when it is remembered that
Zwingli was unexcelled in the classics, a constant
reader of Plato, Aristotle, Cicero and Seneca;
Valerius Maximus he committed to memory, and
Pindar he placed next to the sacred poets. From
his hand-made copy of the New Testament in
Greek, before mentioned, he had learned the Epistles of St. Paul, so as to quote them freely from
memory; and yet so far is he from boasting,
that he seems quite willing to have his brother,
in Saxony, receive the greater honor and praise.

Mosheim, who is supposed to favor Luther in his writings, says, in his History, Vol. III., p. 39 : " The extensive learning and uncommon sagacity of Zwingli, were accompanied with the most heroic intrepidity and resolution. It must even be acknowledged, that this eminent man had perceived some rays of the truth before Luther came to an open rupture with the church of Rome." On this, Dr. Maclaine, the editor, in English, of Dr. Mosheim's History, remarks : " It is well known that Zwingli, from his early years, had been shocked at several of the superstitious practices of the church of Rome; that so early as the year 1516, he began to explain the Scriptures to the people, and to censure, though with great prudence and moderation, the errors of a corrupt church ; and that he had very noble and extensive ideas of a general reformation, at the very time that Luther retained almost the whole system of popery, indulgences excepted. Luther proceeded very slowly to that exemption from the prejudices of education, which Zwingli by the force of an adventurous genius, and an uncommon degree of knowledge and penetration, easily got rid of."

But Zwingli himself sounds the true key-note to this whole subject, where he says : " I began

before a single individual, in our part of the
country, even heard the name of Luther, to
preach the gospel." Christoffel, Zwingli's biog-
rapher, says that the two Reformers began their
work of reformation at about the same time;
and this we think is the truth of the matter;
they began their respective labors for the eman-
cipation of human hearts, and intellects, at
nearly the same time, without any knowledge
of each other's convictions or efforts. The fullness of time had come, when God would purge
the church of her corruptions and errors, and
he called these two great and good men, with
many others, to begin the work of Reform.

Christoffel beautifully adds : "The Spirit of
God moved Luther, at one time like the awful
tempest roaring in a forest of German Oaks ; at
another like the Zephyr soft and gentle, scarcely
agitating the leaves. On the soul of Zwingli,
the Spirit of truth arose in calm majesty like
the sun, slowly and majestically climbing the
blue cerulean over some Swiss mountain ; he
stood immovable in the storms that surrounded
him, like one of his native mountains when the
tempest swathes it round with its girdle of
horrors, or the avalanche leaps from its side
into the abysses beneath."

CHAPTER VII.

LIFE AT THE HERMITAGE OF EINSIEDELN.

WESTWARD from Glarus, and behind the Waggithal mountains, in a romantic valley, lay the village and Cloister of Einsiedeln. We are to follow Zwingli to this place which becomes the center of his reformatory work for some two years, before he enters upon his pastorate at Zurich. Feeling that his mission was now accomplished at Glarus, and acting on the advice of the Master: "When they persecute you in one place, flee to another," he was casting about him, as to what course he ought now to pursue, when Providence opened the way for his engagement at Einsiedeln.

The name of the place suggests its history; the German word "Einsiedelei," signifies life of solitude—hence a Hermitage, or Cloister. Such an institution has been in existence here from the days of Charlemagne. According to tradition, one Meinrad, Count of Sulgen on the

71

Neckar, built a chapel on the "Etzel," a pass some eight miles to the northward, and on the way to lake Zurich, about the middle of the ninth century. His reputation for sanctity, attracted such vast numbers of devotees to his cell, that he was compelled to quit it, and retire to Einsiedeln, where he founded the Abbey, in honor of a miraculous image of the Virgin Mary presented to him by Hildegarde, Abbess of the church of Notre Dame at Zurich. He was assassinated in 861, and his murderers were discovered by two ravens which the holy man had tamed, and which hovered about the men wherever they went, croaking and flapping their dusky wings until the miscreants reached Zurich. The attention of the people was attracted by this singular circumstance, and the result was that the men were arrested, tried, and immediately executed.

The reputation of St. Meinrad increased so rapidly after his death, that a Benedictine Abbey was founded on the spot where his cell had stood. The legend relates that when the Bishop of Constance was about to consecrate the church, on the fourteenth of September, 948, heavenly voices announced to him at midnight that the Saviour himself, surrounded by his angels, had already performed the ceremony. A bull of Pope Leo VII. confirmed the miracle, and accorded plenary indulgences to all who should perform the pilgrimage to "Our Lady of the Hermits." The offerings of the crowd of worshippers were a source of great wealth to the Abbey. The Emperor Rudolph of Hapsburg created its Abbot, Prince of the Empire in 1274, and this dignitary lived in almost regal magnificence, exercising supreme authority over an extensive district.

At the time when Zwingli was about to leave Glarus, Conrad of Rechberg was the Abbot of Einsiedeln, a man of generous impulses, and of great independence of character. He was a pious, excellent, upright man under whose monk's cloak beat as warm and generous a heart as ever throbbed under a coat of mail. In his youth he had been forced to join the monks, by selfish relatives, who paid him visits, now that he had risen to be Abbot-Prince of Einsiedeln. These visits were often made with the view of obtaining some favor in the gift of the Abbot. It is characteristic of the man that on one occasion he said to them: "You have stuck a cowl upon my head to my soul's risk and peril, and I must be a monk, while you ride about as country squires. But, my good people, since you have made a poor monk of me, don't come here begging anything, but just return the road by which you came."

As might be expected from the character of the man, he held very independent views of the outward forms of worship, which in that day were honored as the grounds of salvation. He was once reproached by the visitors of the church for neglecting to say mass. He replied: "Although I am master here in my own convent, and could send you away with a very short answer, yet I will tell you plainly what I think of the mass. If the Lord Jesus Christ be really in the host (wafer), I know not how very highly you esteem yourselves; one thing I know, that I a poor monk, am not worthy to look upon Him, not to speak of offering Him up in sacrifice to the eternal God. If, however, He be not present there, woe's me, if I hold up bread to the people before the Lord our God, and call upon them to worship bread. I shall, if God will, so act and so preside over my God's house that I may be able to answer to myself before Him and the world. As I have no need of you, please to return the way you came; you are dismissed."

He was also impatient of doctrinal discussions;

and once when Leo Juda was discussing some
subject, at table, with the administrator of the
Abbey, he exclaimed: "Let me put an end to
your disputings:—I say with David,—'Have
mercy upon me, O God! according to thy loving-
kindness: Enter not into judgment with thy
servant!'—and I want nothing more." In fact
Abbot Conrad was more fond of the chase, and
of his fine breed of horses than he was of the
discussions of the priests; yet he was an upright
man, and his bluntness, was but the utterance
of candor in an age when the church needed reformation.

As he was now advanced in years, he had
appointed Baron Theobald Geroldseck administrator of the Abbey. He was of a mild
character, sincerely pious and fond of learning.
He thought to elevate the standing of his institution by calling around him a company of
learned men; and hearing that Zwingli was
about to leave Glarus, he invited him to Einsiedeln. Accordingly an agreement was entered
into on the 14th of April, 1516, in consequence
of which Zwingli undertook the office of preacher
and pastor, assistant to the people's priest.
Zwingli was not moved to leave Glarus for hope
of temporal gain, for in his new capacity he was

to receive only 20 florins at the quarter fastings, a trifle from the penny collections, and confessional, with the promise of a full pastorate in the future, while he enjoyed a free seat at the common table.

He was moved to take the place therefore partly because of the French opposition already mentioned, at Glarus; but more particularly with the hope that he would here have more time for study and conference with learned men, and be able to exercise a greater influence upon his fellow-men. When it was known that he was to leave Glarus, the greater portion of his people were filled with sorrow and regret. His enemies no longer spoke against him; and his friends gathered around him with the greatest enthusiasm. The people insisted that the pastoral relation should not be severed, and in hope that he might again return, his official standing was continued for some years, while the pastoral work was done by his vicar or assistant.

It was under these circumstances, therefore, that Zwingli wended his way down the narrow valley of the Linth, through which he had passed ten years before, when he came to receive this, his first charge. Arriving at the shore of Zurich lake, his way ran southward, over the Etzel pass, where once stood the hut of the hermit Meinard, and from thence down the mountain side to the romantic green valley of the Alpbach, where stood the stately buildings of the Abbey, which, for a time would be his home.

Here Zwingli was received with open arms by Geroldseck, who with Francis Zink, and John Oechslin, were afterwards bound to him with the ties of a most intimate friendship. In this company, with time for study, conference and meditation, he made rapid advances in the divine life. His friends knew how to appreciate his scholarship, and soon imbibed his views touching the need of reformation in the church. He brought with him the settled conviction that the Word of God is the only sure directory for faith and practice, and Christ the only way of salvation. He experienced in his own heart how precious and dear that saying is: "Jesus Christ came into the world to save sinners." To his friends he gave the advice, that they should study the Fathers as he had done, for the better understanding of the Holy Scriptures; yet he added: "With God's grace, the day will soon come, that neither Jerome, nor any other, will be an authority in matters of faith, but the Bible alone."

The fruit of his teachings soon began to appear. Geroldseck announced to the nuns in the cloister of Fahr, that instead of daily drawling over the mass-songs in their usual heedless manner, they were to read the New Testament in the German tongue; at the same time, that those who felt themselves burdened by their vows, had liberty to return to their relatives. Those who remained were to lead, true to their vows, a virtuous and holy life. Accordingly, many of the nuns returned to their homes.

At this time also, Zwingli made good use of his little pocket edition of the New Testament, which he had previously written out with his own hand, as already stated, in the Greek characters. Daubigne says: "He learnt by heart the whole of the Epistles; then the remaining books of the New Testament; and after that portions of the Old." Unlike Luther who came to his true religious experience by a shock, Zwingli seems, from the first, to have found light from his gradual, and growing acquaintance with the Scriptures. His former extravagant fondness for the classical authors, was now absorbed in his glowing admiration for inspired writings; and even the writings of the Fathers became less esteemed by him, except as they served to throw light upon the pages of inspiration.

This period was to Zwingli what the life in the wilderness was to John the Baptist, or the sojourn of the prophet in Horeb was to Elijah, or, considered in an earthly point of view, what the forty days of fasting and temptation were to our Saviour. Here, in the Abbey, Zwingli had leisure to pursue those investigations which lay so near to his heart, and here he gave himself to study and prayer. He also prepared himself with care for the pulpit. He studied first of all, in the original, the section which the church prescribed to be read in Latin. He then commented upon the passage according to its sense, and made the practical application of it, without suffering himself to be fettered, in the least degree, either by the dogmas or the prejudices of the church.

According to his own statement, Zwingli dated his conversion from the time he read the poem of Erasmus, to which allusion has already been made. In reference to that event he thus wrote in 1523: "I shall not withhold from you, dear brethren in Christ, how it was I arrived at the conviction and firm faith, that we require no other mediator but Christ, and that none but Christ alone can mediate between God and man. I read, eight or nine years ago, (1514?) a poem of Erasmus, in which the complaint is made, that men do not seek all good from Him, who is the source of all good. Thereon I reflected, why do we seek help of the creature." That was the dawn of his true religious experience, and now at Einsiedeln, his convictions were deepened, and so his became the path of the just, " as the shining light, that shineth, more and more, unto the perfect day."

But as the light of God was shining upon his path it revealed to him the fact that a dark and dangerous superstition had spread itself over the Abbey of Einsiedeln. The tradition of that angelic consecration of the Cloister, in the tenth century when, at midnight, heavenly voices announcnounced to the Bishop, that the Saviour himself with his retinue of saints had already consecrated it, still held its power over the minds of the people. The image of the Virgin, said to have been presented to the monk Meinard, by the Abbess at Zurich, was exhibited within the shrine of the Abbey church, and believed to perform wonders for those who brought offerings, and prayed before it. They were taught that they would be forgiven and saved through Mary's intercessions.

Over the gateway of the magnificent abbey, where every pilgrim would not fail to see them, were inscribed in golden letters, these words: " Hic est plena remissio omnium peccatorum a culpa et poena." *i. e.,* " Here is full remission for the guilt and penalty of all sin." Daubigne says: "A multitude of pilgrims, from all parts of Christendom, flocked to Einsiedeln, that they might obtain this grace for their pilgrimage. The church, the abbey, the whole valley, was crowded on the occasion of the festival of the Virgin, with her devout worshippers. But it was especially on the grand festival of the angelic " Consecration," that the crowd thronged the hermitage. Long files to the number of several thousands of both sexes, climbed the steep sides of the mountain leading to the oratory, singing hymns, or counting the beads of their chaplets. These devout pilgrims forced their way into the church, believing themselves nearer to God there than anywhere else."

We need not be surprised to learn that the spirit of Zwingli was stirred within him at this sight. He was now compelled to witness frequent scenes of this kind. It was not an easy matter to antagonize such an extensive custom of pilgrimage, and false devotion, as that which was

firmly seated in Einsiedeln at that time. And
Zwingli was to receive his living, in part, from
the proceeds of this extensive patronage resulting from the attendance of the thousands of persons, from all parts of the land, at the annual
festivals. The reader has by this time learned
enough of the character of Zwingli, however, to
infer that no prestige of past custom, no thought
of his personal interests would hinder him from
speaking out plainly against these abuses. The
extent of the evil, and the power of superstition
in its aid, with which Zwingli had to contend,
and which he successfully arrested, may be inferred from the fact, that after his death, these
pilgrimages to Einsiedeln were renewed, and
are continued till this very day.

In 1798 the greater part of the treasures were
carried away by the French, but the monks had
rescued the image of the Virgin, and kept it in
the Tyrol; and when danger was past, they returned with it to Einsiedeln again. Since that
time, pilgrimages to this shrine have been resumed. In 1710 the number of pilgrims
amounted to 260,000; it is now said to average
150,000 annually. On high festivals an immense
crowd flock hither from all parts of Switzerland,
from Bavaria and Swabia, the Black Forest,

Alsace, Lorraine, and even more distant regions. The greater proportion belong to the poorer classes, many of whom are paid for their pious services by the rich, who thus perform an act of devotion by deputy. With the exception of Loreto in Italy, Compostella in Spain, Mariazell in Styria, Einsiedeln attracts more pilgrims than any other shrine. Like Delphi and Ephesus, in their day, this shrine has gathered its thousands of pilgrims, from generation to generation. Over seven hundred workmen are daily employed in making relics to sell to the pilgrims, by one establishment; which traffic like that of Demetrius, who made silver shrines for Diana at Ephesus brings " no small gain to the craftsmen." Acts 19 : 24.

CHAPTER VIII.

PREACHING TO PILGRIMS AT EINSIEDELN.

THE modern tourist who visits Einsiedeln, will find a large open space between the houses and the church, in which stands a black marble fountain, surmounted by an image of the Virgin, from which the pilgrims are wont to drink. Under the Arcades, which form a semicircular approach to the church on the right and left, as well as in the square itself, there are numerous stalls for the sale of missals, images of saints, rosaries, medals, crucifixes, and similar articles. Within the church itself, in the nave, and separated from the rest of the building stands the chapel of the virgin, of black marble. This is the Sanctum Sanctorum, to which pilgrims pay particular reverence. A grate protects the front, through which, illuminated by a solitary lamp, a small image of the Virgin and Child is visible, richly attired, and adorned with crowns of gold and precious stones.

84

Judging from the existing power which this shrine has over the minds of the more credulous members of the church of Rome; and remembering that in the days of Zwingli this superstition of the pilgrimage was at its height, we can imagine what a task lay before him if he should lift up his voice in opposition to the custom which so delighted the pilgrims, and brought in such large revenues to the Abbey. We must also bear in mind the fact, that in this year of 1516, there was no general movement of reform, of which tidings had come to this part of Switzerland. It was not until the following year that Luther broke away from the papacy, by nailing his ninety-five theses to the church door in Wittemberg. If, therefore, Zwingli attacks the abuses of the pilgrimages, he does so without any evidence that he will receive any sympathy whatever, except from the little circle of his intimate friends. But on the other hand he knows that his Abbot, bluff old Conrad, has no heart in the miserable system, and he knows that right, and truth, are on his side.

Zwingli was not a blind enthusiast; he felt the gravity of his position, just as much as Luther did at the Diet of Worms. He had just as much at stake as Luther had, *i. e.*, his life.

And he thus wrote: " Once for all, the spirit must be so consecrated to God, that it may hang inseparably on right, truth, and God, even to the loss of outward means, and life itself; once for all the die must be cast, and death looked steadily in the face, for the truth's sake, and the soul nerved against every attack of the flesh, the world, and Satan." He accordingly raised his voice against the delusions here practiced under his eyes. Says Christoffel: " His soul indeed, burned with a holy indignation at the dishonor done to the name of God, and the Saviour. He grieved for a people who, instead of finding forgiveness for their sins, entangled themselves faster and faster in the net of Satan."

The same author gives an excellent account of Zwingli's preaching at Einsiedeln. " God," the preacher cried, " is everywhere present, and wherever we call upon Him, in spirit and in truth, He answers us in the words, Here I am !" Those then, who bind the grace of God to particular localities, are altogether foolish and perverse ; nay, it is not only foolish and perverse so to do, but anti-Christian, for they represent the grace of God as more easily to be obtained, and cheaper, in one place than in another, which is nothing but to limit the grace of God, and take it captive, not letting it be known how free it is. God is in every part of the earth where He is called upon, present and ready to hear our prayers, and to help us. Wherefore St. Paul says: 'I will therefore—that men pray everywhere . . . . In like manner also the women,' 1st Timothy, 2: 8, 9, 'that is, we are to know that God is present, and hears us, when He is called upon, and that He is not more gracious in one place than in another.'"

Of course the utterances of Zwingli suffer much through the medium of a translation, but the truths he proclaims, are unmistakeable, and they must have fallen with startling effect upon the ears of that people, who had been accustomed only to hear the efficiency of the absolution, to be obtained just there, and the miraculous power of the image of the Virgin, extolled. Zwingli continued: "Christ calls such people as bind God to this, or that place, false Christians, that is Anti-Christs. 'There shall arise false Christs, and false prophets and deceive many,' Matt. 24: 24. O God, who else is a hypocritical Christian but the Pope, who exalts himself in the place of Christ, and says he has his power ; so he binds God to Rome, and other sanctuaries. Thus they bring money in enormous quantities

to enrich holy places, which in case of need,
might well be applied to our temporal advantage.   And just in such places is more wanton-
ness and vice perpetrated than anywhere else.
He who ascribes to man the power to forgive
sins blasphemes God.   And great evil has
sprung from this source, so that some whose
eyes the Popes have blinded, have imagined
they had their sins forgiven by sinful men.   In
this manner God Himself has been hid from
them.   To ascribe to man the power to forgive
sins is idolatry! What is idolatry, but the as-
cription of the divine honor to man, or the giving to the creature that which is God's."

Surely this was a bold utterance for any priest
to make; evidently he takes the risk of suffering what Huss suffered, that is death.   But he
is not through yet; he refers to the fact mentioned in the Scriptures that the people at Lys-
tra, would do sacrifice to Paul, and Barnabas as
gods, to which they replied: "Sirs, why do ye
these things? We also are men of like passions
with you. . . Turn unto the living God." "What
think you, the Virgin Mary would say, if she
were to witness this, that men sought from her,
that which alone is God's to give? Think you
not that she would say: 'O senseless, deluded

men, all the honor I have comes from God! He has been gracious to me, and made me a Virgin, and the mother among all women. But I am no goddess, nor any source of blessing; God alone is that Fountain, who has ordained that all good should come to you through My Son. By attributing to me that which alone is God's, ye poor mortals attempt to change the power and government of God. For verily since the beginning of the world, He has given to no creature such a power as that any should flee to it for succor as if it were God. I am no god, therefore seek not from me that which is God's alone to give." . . . . . "The greatest honor of Mary is her Son; it is likewise her greatest honor that we rightly know Him, and that we love Him above all things, and that we manifest our eternal gratitude to Him for His act of mercy in redeeming us. If ye will honor her then, follow her purity, and her steadfast faith."

This was the burden of Zwingli's preaching, at the festival of the angel-consecration, in 1517, and at Pentecost, 1518, before great crowds of pilgrims. Great was the impression it made upon the pilgrims. Some fled in terror from the scene, others hovered between the faith of their fathers and the doctrine that was to give them peace; others turned to Christ with their whole hearts, and returned to their homes bearing back with them the tapers, and gifts intended for the image of the Virgin. On their way they met many other pilgrims, on their way to the shrine, to whom they related what had taken place; and the doctrine of Zwingli, that: "*Christ Alone saves us, and He saves everywhere.*" Pilgrims, as they heard this, turned back without bringing their pilgrimage to a close. The fame of Zwingli, the bold and uncompromising advocate of truth, resounded through the towns and villages of Switzerland, Suabia, and Alsace. "In truth," says Daubigne, "an universal astonishment took possession of men's minds at the sound of the eloquent priest's sermons."

Many learned men were drawn to Einsiedeln, to hear this new prophet in the wilderness, among whom was Dr. Hedio, then the preacher at Basel; who heard Zwingli preach at the Pentecost festival, 1518, from Luke 5: 24, "The Son of man hath power on earth to forgive sins." Hedio was so deeply affected by the discourse that he afterwards begged Zwingli to receive him into the number of his friends, or at least to let him be the shadow of one. Of the sermon he wrote: " It was beautiful, fundamental, dignified, comprehensive, searching, truly evangelical, reminding one, in force of language and of spirit, of the old fathers of the church." Hedio longed to go to the preacher and open his heart to him; he lingered about the Abbey without daring to make advances, restrained, as he tells us, by a sort of superstitious fear. Mounting his horse, he slowly departed from the hermitage, looking back on a spot which held so great a treasure, with the warmest regrets.

The number of pilgrims was now greatly diminished; that great stream which had been flowing to this spot for centuries, bearing with it the choicest gifts of the people, seemed to be suddenly checked. And it is recorded that the effect of Zwingli's preaching was, at one time, so great that the monks left their cells on the occasion of an anniversary festival, and the abbey was deserted for a considerable time.

It was to be expected that a part of the monks, at least, would be indignant at the course pursued by Zwingli. This was indeed the case; many of the monks were scandalized, but the Abbot, and Geroldseck protected and encouraged the orator. And Zwingli did not confine his ef-

forts to the pulpit; to Cardinal Schinner he said:
" Every one knows that, the faith and practice
of Christians have, by a gradual declension,
departed very widely from sound evangelical
doctrine, and it is undeniable that, some very
great reformation of laws and manners is abso-
lutely necessary. If we do not give vent to the
water, the dam will be broken in by force."

To the papal legate Zwingli said: "I have
both by word and deed witnessed to mighty
cardinals, prelates, and bishops, of the errors
in doctrine that are abroad, and warned and
counselled them to remove abuses, or that they
themselves would perish in a more dreadful
revolution. I have told Cardinal Von Sitten at
Einsiedeln, (in 1519); and afterwards, in plain
language, that the papacy has a false foundation
and maintained it by unanswerable passages of
Holy Writ. And he replied, that if he was restored to power, he would see to it that the ar-
rogance and fraud of the Bishop of Rome be
brought to light, and put an end to. To another
legate he said: " I am resolved from hencefor-
ward to preach the pure Gospel to the people,
without regard to the statutes of men, whereby
without doubt, the papacy will not be a little
shaken."

The natural inference would be, after reading all this, that the dignitaries of the church would proceed to silence the bold preacher. But it did not suit their purpose, to put him under banns at present. They needed his help against the French enlistments; and they hoped to gain him back again to the papacy. Thus they pursued a directly opposite course from that pursued against Luther. As Zwingli was more moderate in his course, although equally as firm, he gave less offence to men's minds than the Saxon monk; he trusted to the power of truth for the results. Far from denouncing in wholesale terms, the dignitaries of the church, he continued long on friendly terms with them. They treated him with respect on account of his learning and talents, and also on account of the influence which they foresaw such a man would be likely to have in a republic.

Daubigne says : " Rome sought to intimidate Luther by solemn judgments; and to win Zwingli by her favors. Against one she hurled excommunications; to the other she cast her gold and splendors. They were two different methods for attaining the same end, and sealing the daring lips which presumed, in opposition to the Pope's pleasure, to proclaim the Word of

God in Germany and Switzerland. The last device was the most skillfully conceived, but neither was successful. The enlarged heart of the preachers of the Gospel were shown to be above the reach of vengeance, or seduction.

Zwingli was now the recipient of a new honor from the Pope ; he was created Acolyte-chaplain of the papal-chair. The grand document of investiture ran as follows : " Distinguished by his virtues and great merits, he deserves, in the eyes of the Pope and the holy apostolic chair, a recognition of his great learning, and some distinguished mark of paternal approbation." He was counselled to go on improving, and advancing from good to better, and by his merits to incline the Pope, and the Legate, to grant farther testimonies in his favor. The ladder was thus planted at the feet of the Reformer, by which he might mount to the highest honors the world had to bestow ; but Zwingli chose the crown of thorns and the cross of Christ, before worldly glory. He gave up even the little stipend allowed him, for the purchase of books, and thus turned away from all the earthly profits, which now might so easily have been his.

The promised reforms under Cardinal Schinner, and others, were not carried out ; so Zwingli appealed to Landenburg, then Bishop of Constance, to stay the corruption of the Church in his own diocese, and recommend to his clergy the preaching of the pure Gospel. But the Bishop showed as little will, or power, in the cause of church reform, as the Pope and his cardinals, although he had previously maintained strong language on the subject of the degeneracy of the church. Zwingli sent his message in a letter. The Bishop read it, and only tossed it aside with the remark: "Convent preachers are not my advisers, when the holy father orders a reform, it will be time enough to begin it."

Still Zwingli persevered in his good work, with frankness and earnestness, always testifying for the truth and looking for a better time to come. On one occasion when he was walking through the romantic valley at the Hermitage, with his friend Capito, he said: "The papacy must fall." To which the friend replied: "The sooner the better." And yet Capito himself, in after time, lost heart under the discouragements of the bitter opposition, while Zwingli, with the cheerfulness characteristic of him, persevered to the end.

The freedom of the church was not to be won by any faint-hearted reformers; only those who set their hearts as a flint, as did Luther and Zwingli; who persevered, when all around was discouraging to common men, won the true reformer's crown. They made mistakes, it is true; they were not infallible; they may have been saddened, and often pained, at the apparent indifference of those who should have stood with them, but with each defeat they rose to higher planes of action; and when, at last, they fell asleep in death, others arose who faithfully carried on the issue, until victory was achieved. Their names stand written on the fair pages of history, which record the acts of the great and good. And as Coleridge beautifully writes:

"Goodness and greatness are not means, but ends.
　Hath he not always treasures, always friends,
　The good great man? Three treasures-love, and light,
　And calm thoughts, equable as infant's breath;
　And three fast friends more sure than day or night—
　Himself, his Maker, and the angel Death?"

CHAPTER IX.

A CONFLICT WITH SAMSON.

ONE day in the month of August, 1518, there appeared upon the St. Gottard pass a strange-looking procession. It was a sort of caravan, or resembled, more nearly, a band of strolling actors. In advance went two men, making a proclamation, and directing the attention of the people, who looked on with amazement, to the interests that were to be presented to them by the character who had charge of the enterprise. The individual who was thus heralded came on apace. He was a monk from Italy, of the Carmelite order, barefooted and covered with dust. His name was Samson, and he had in his custody an immense quantity of papers, which, he took care to explain, contained the signature of the Pope. These papers, or certificates, were called indulgences.

As soon as he arrived in a village he made his proclamation: that "for the required amount of

7   97

money " he would dispose of these indulgences to any one who would purchase them. Strange as it seems to us now, the poor people, who made their living by hard toil, and frequent exposure to the rigorous climate of Switzerland, who followed the life of the herdsman, or the farmer, crowded around this man, and began to pour their hard-earned money into his coffers. And what was it that they hoped to gain by this investment? The complete pardon of all their sins. In their haste to secure the coveted prize, they contended with one another as to who should be first to part with his little pittance, saved up for the needs of the coming winter, and hand it all over to the agent of the Pope.

Let us not smile at their eagerness or their convictions. Fostered in poverty and ignorance, they had been trained up from childhood to the belief that authorized men could absolve them from the guilt and penalty of sin. They are rather to be pitied than blamed for their readiness to give even their last penny for such a boon. Many pilgrims went to Rome each year that they might receive these certificates; and now, the better to accommodate their needs (for many of them were too poor to make a pilgrimage to Rome), the Pope kindly sent forth his commissioned agent to dispose of these indulgences at their very doors. Why should they not, therefore, show their appreciation of this favor by patronizing the wares ready to hand?

The purchaser had a double advantage offered him: he might secure the pardon of his own sins, and also deliver the souls of his deceased friends from the pains of purgatory. The money thus obtained was named Peter's Pence, and was devoted to the cost of building the great St. Peter's Church at Rome. It was the ambition of Pope Leo X, then seated in the papal chair, to erect a structure that would outshine all other churches in its size and magnificence. And when the funds ran short he sent forth these agents, as other popes had done before him, and thus he realized a handsome increase. The passage of four centuries since has made this traffic seem very odious to us; but at that time it was only a brave man that dared to raise an objection.

Samson made his way towards the canton where Einsiedeln was situated, known as the Schwitz. Here he began to proclaim: "I can forgive all sins; heaven and hell stand under my dominion; and I sell the merits of Jesus Christ to each and every one who is willing to pay in

ready money for an absolution." Wherever he
came Samson erected a red cross in one of the
churches as the sign of his office, which he al-
leged was equally efficacious with the cross
upon which the Saviour suffered. He caused his
arrival, and his business, and the time of his stay
to be announced from the pulpits, and then
proceeded with his traffic. The rich were taxed
in proportion to their wealth, and obliged to
pay high prices for the pardons, and the
poor were urged to keep in the background
lest they crowd out the wealthy patrons.

At last the tidings of these doings reached the
ears of Zwingli. On the next Sabbath he openly
attacked the whole system. He said: "Jesus
Christ, the Son of God, has said, 'Come unto
me all that labor and are heavy laden, and I
will give you rest.' It is audacious folly and
shameless impudence to say: 'Run to Rome,
buy a ticket of absolution, give this to the
monks, that to the priests; if you do so, then I
pronounce you free from all sin!' No; Jesus
Christ is the only sacrifice, the only gift, the
only way." This bold utterance was not without effect; it only needed one to stand out in
opposition to such a traffic, when many others
would take heart to decry it. But there must

always be a first one, like Luther, who opposed
this same abuse under Tetzel in Saxony, and
here again Zwingli, in Switzerland. If the
soldiers at Concord fired a shot that was heard
around the world, these two Reformers, without
arms, inaugurated a revolution that never has,
and never can, go backward.

From that time forward Samson found difficulty in the prosecution of his errand in the
Schwitz. He hastily withdrew from the canton
and retreated to points where the clarion voice
of Zwingli had not yet penetrated. And yet the
influence followed him, and seriously hindered
the success of his efforts. The people throughout
the canton began to say : " Samson is a cheat and
a robber." He feared an uproar, dreaded to meet
Zwingli, and left hurriedly for another canton.

Samson turned back, first to Zúg, where he
continued his traffic, and then no doubt thinking
it safe to place a considerable distance between
Zwingli and himself, for the present, he went on
to Lucerne. From Lucerne he went to Ober-
land, and arrived at length in the vicinity of
Bern. But before speaking of his doings there,
we will mention an incident connected with his
visit to the Schwitz.

There was a citizen there of good standing,

who had patronized the monk to such an extent
that he became suddenly reduced, with his family, to extreme poverty. In his extremity he
applied to Zwingli, stating that he was unable
to satisfy his hunger and that of his children.
Now it might be presumed that many would
upbraid him with his folly in giving away his
living for the worthless indulgences. Not so
with Zwingli; his was too true a Christian heart
to permit him to adopt such a course. Daubigne
says: "Zwingli could give when Rome would
take, and he was as ready to do good works as
he was to oppose those who taught that they
were means by which we are saved. He daily
supplied Stapfer with support. "It is God,"
said he, intent on taking no credit to himself,
"it is God who begets charity in the believer,
and gives at once the first thought, the resolve,
and the work itself." The grateful man never
forgot his friend in need, and four years after
this, when he was the honored Secretary of the
Canton, he turned to Zwingli, seeking that
which alone can supply the wants of the soul,
and said: "Since it was you who once supplied
my temporal wants, how much more may I expect you may point me to that which shall satisfy the famine of my soul."

The authorities at Bern were not disposed to admit Samson within their city. But through the good offices of some who were friendly to him, he at last succeeded in spreading his wares in St. Vincent's Church. He was encouraged at his success in getting a hearing, and became very bold in his proclamation. To the rich he said: "Here are indulgences on parchment for one crown." And to the poor he said : "There are absolutions on common paper for three half-pence only." One incident at Bern is related that seems hardly credible. It is the case of Jacob Von Stein, a knight of high standing, who came galloping up to the place where Samson was engaged one day, and asked for absolution for himself, his five hundred followers, his ancestors, and his whole family. The horse on which the knight was seated pleased the monk, and a bargain was soon made, whereby the wholesale indulgence was granted, and the horse was led away to the monk's stable. Samson played the part of a giant here indeed, and forced an aged man, who was very worthy, and greatly respected by all, to fall upon his knees before him, and ask his pardon, for having let fall a word in criticism of the system of indulgences.

The Bernese, as we remarked above, seem to have been a merry people, and it may be, on this account that Samson reserved his greatest deed, at this place, till the last. The monk took his place upon the high altar in the church, and had Henry Lupulus (Wolf), Zwingli's former teacher, for his interpreter. " When the wolf and the fox come abroad together," said a good man to another minister, "the wisest plan for you is to gather your sheep and geese, with all speed, into a place of safety." To such remarks Samson paid no heed, if, indeed, he heard them ; but in a loud voice he called out: " Fall on your knees, repeat three paternosters and three Ave-Marias, and you will instantly be as pure as you were at the moment of your baptism." The people fell on their knees, and Samson cried out: " I deliver from the torments of purgatory and hell the souls of all the people of Bern who have departed this life, whatsoever may have been the manner or the place of their death." To us such a scene would be shocking in the extreme. Such a great change has the Reformation produced in the thought of the world that, we may hope, such conduct may never be repeated.

Samson had been very successful at Bern,

and went away with a well-filled treasury, and presenting quite a different appearance from the poor display he made when he first came over the St. Gottard pass. He came as far as Baden, and forming a procession he marched around the graveyard. While thus engaged he cast his eyes toward heaven, while his aids chanted the hymn for the dead; and pretending that he saw the liberated souls flying up from the churchyard toward heaven, he cried out: " Behold, they fly ! " A rude but effective rebuke was administered to him, by a man in the neighborhood, who climbed up in the church steeple and ripping open a pillow of feathers let them scatter downward through the air, exclaiming: " Behold, they fly ! " This had the effect of bringing his traffic into ridicule, and greatly angered the monk. He was only prevented from taking vengeance on the man by hearing that he was, at times, disordered in his intellect.

Afterward he appeared at Bremgarten, where the Rev. Dean Bullinger, whose son afterward became a noted reformer, opposed his objectional mission. No sooner had he settled himself at the hotel than Bullinger came to him and forbade the sale of indulgences within his charge. " Here are the Pope's bulls," said

Samson, " open your church to me." As he did not have the authority of the bishop of that canton, Bullinger said: " I will suffer no one under the color of such letters to squeeze the purses of my people." Samson said: "The pope is above the bishop. I charge you not to deprive your flock of so marvellous a grace." The Dean replied: " Were it to cost me my life, I will not open my church. Samson then became fiercely angry, and said: " In the name of the Pope I pronounce against thee the greater excommunication, nor will I grant thee absolution until you have paid three hundred ducats." But the Dean was true to his position and said: " I am prepared to answer for myself before my lawful judges. As for thee and thy excommunication, I have nothing to do with either." The position of Zwingli was beginning to have a wholesome effect in many parts of Switzerland, and in the end was destined to drive Samson back again over the Alps, but not until they had come into close quarters once more in the new field wherein our Reformer is now to be stationed.

CHAPTER X.

FROM THE HERMITAGE TO THE CITY.

THE time had now arrived when Zwingli was to take his departure from the usually quiet retreat of Einsiedeln. His work at this point, had been attended with great success; he had here challenged the grave abuses which had crept into the church, and for the time, had turned backward that tide of deluded pilgrims who, year by year, for ages past had swept over the Etzel-Pass, to worship, "Our Lady of the Eremites." He had here forged one sentence, which the Christian ages should ever repeat as a sufficient answer to all theories of religious worship at the shrine of some reputed saint: "*Christ alone saves us, and He saves everywhere.*"

Here also he had given the true watchword against the pardon of pope and priest, in the words of Christ Himself: "Come unto ME all ye that labor, and I will give you rest." He had made many enemies it is true, but he had

107

also made many true friends, and he had the witness in his bosom that he had discharged his duty.

About this time a vacancy occurred in the Cathedral church at Zurich. The rising reputation of Zwingli led his friends to suggest his name for the place. But no sooner was his name proposed than his enemies, of the papacy, began to make opposition, and to thrust forward candidates of their own views. Attached to the cathedral itself was a college of canons, connected with which, was a school placed under the care of Oswald Myconius, Zwingli's friend. The teacher used his utmost endeavor to have Zwingli appointed. What a blessing it would be, thought Oswald, to Zurich, to have this man to fill the place ! Zwingli's manners and appearance were prepossessing; he was already remarked for his eloquence, and distinguished among all the confederated Swiss for his brilliant genius.

Myconius spoke of him to the provost of the chapter, Felix Frey, who was favorably disposed. Other men of authority were consulted, and many signified their willingness to vote for the late pastor at Einsiedeln. And a number of citizens, who had heard Zwingli's

eloquent discourses, on the occasion of the pilgrimages, spoke in his favor.

But the opposition were active also, and
brought forward one Lorenzo Fabel, a Suabian,
and a strong advocate of the papacy, and had
him officiate at Zurich as a candidate. But his
record as to morality was not good, and gave
rise to objections on the part of many. All
Zurich was astir with interest regarding the
matter. Myconious wrote to Zwingli of Fabel,
and said that the man was what his name im-
ported a Fable. And on receipt of the tidings
that the Suabian was actually elected, Zwingli
wrote to his friend : "True it is then, that no
prophet is honored in his own country, since a
Suabian is preferred before a Swiss." But the
report was without foundation ; the previous
bad conduct of the man had prevented his election, and Zwingli might yet be chosen.

Among the objections raised against Zwingli,
by his opponents was that there were rumors
against the character of the man dating from
his pastorate at Glarus. It seems likely that
these rumors were set afloat in order to offset
the well known licentiousness of Fabel. When
Zwingli was written to on the subject, he frankly replied that he had been tempted, and in the

impulse of youth had been led away into improper
conduct at one time, which he had sincerely re-
pented of, and for which he hoped he was forgiven. And we can the more readily excuse a
weakness, on the part of Zwingli, when we
remember the rude customs of the times, and
the teachings which, for many generations, had
been tolerated by the church of Rome. The
result of the exciting canvas for the pulpit at
Zurich was that Zwingli received seventeen, out
of twenty-four votes, and was declared elected.

When it was known that he was to leave
Einsiedeln, his friends, the Abbot and Geroldseck, with the little coterie that had gathered
about him, and had hung upon his teachings
with joy, became very sad at the thought of
parting from him, and yet they rejoiced that
such a wide field would now be opened to him,
and wished him all success. Even the Council
of Schwitz, transmitted to him an address, in
which they styled him " their reverend, learned,
and very gracious Master, and worthy friend."
And they added: " Although we are, in part,
grieved by your departure from among us, yet,
on the other hand, we rejoice with you in all
that ministers to your honor and advantage."

Nor were these the only marks of apprecia-

tion bestowed upon him. The people at Win-
terthur had, a short time before this, invited
him to become their pastor; and his former
flock at Glarus wished him to return to them.
He did make them a visit before entering upon
his new field of labor. He resigned the honorary pastorate which they had persuaded him to
retain hitherto, and had the pleasure of seeing
his friend Dingauer, whom he had recommended
to them, chosen as his successor. In like manner he was asked to name a successor at Einsiedeln, and recommended Leo Juda, and he was
warmly welcomed there. Thus was his character vindicated by those who had been near to
him during his entire ministerial life, from the
charge of his enemies, who opposed his election
at Zurich.

Having thus taken a friendly leave of his
former friends, he turns his face towards his
new field of labor. He goes with the kind re-
membrance of many affectionate hearts, and
with a record that time can never efface. Once
more he climbs the heights of the Etzel, and the
blue waters of lake Zurich, stretch out before
him, at the farther end of which, lies the city
he is now to enter as his future home. It was
a December morning; a gray fog hung upon

the hilltops, while the sun's rays were glinting along the icy, and snow crowned, mountain peaks in the distance. In the struggles of the morning sun, with the cloudy vapors, he beheld, says Christoffel: "an image of that conflict with the powers of darkness which he himself was now hastening to wage." And as he sailed on over the waters of the lake, these were the thoughts which filled his mind, and which he reduced to writing: "As the heaven, peaceful and clear, encircles with its blue canopy high over head, the whole earth, though lightnings and tempests be beneath; thus the truly wise man, the Christian, rises above all storms and tempests. If you weigh all, you will find that the principle of good is stronger than that of evil, and that in the end, virtue overcomes vice. True wisdom obtains the mastery over iniquity; for at the moment when this has reached its culminating point, the divine power seizes it and hurls it into the abyss. Herein God shows His power."

The lake of Zurich is a lovely sheet of water, lovely even in that land of charming inland seas, and lofty mountains. It is twenty-five and a half miles long, and two and a half wide. It is the shape of a crescent; or rather like one of those long winding horns on which the Swiss are accustomed to play their wild melodies, which ring among the mountain peaks, with many playful echoes, as the herdsmen follow their cattle up to the lofty summits, when summer suns have worn away the past winter's snow. The indented shores, the cultivated slopes, the orchards, and farm houses, with here and there a pretty hamlet set down by the water's edge, form the outlines of a pleasing landscape

Lake Zurich is fed by the Linth, the stream which, it will be remembered, flows down from Glarus to the lake of Wallenstadt; and so, by the ancient bed of the Maag, these waters flow on towards Zurich, which stands at the farther, or northern end. The outlet of the lake, Zurich is the river Limmat, a broad, clear, flowing stream, which speeds on its way northward to the Rhine, bearing with it, in its swift passage along the streets of Zurich, and down through fertile valleys beyond, the pure waters of the Glarus hills. And so, we may add, the reformer who began his great work at Glarus, is now on his way to bring the glad-tidings of a free Gospel to Zurich; whence it will flow out through many valleys, and by many mountain-sides, into various other lands, to make glad the hearts of the people.

8

Zwingli entered Zurich on the 27th day of
December and went immediately to the hotel
of " The Hermits," where for the present he
tarried, and where he was waited upon by many
of the citizens who would bid him welcome in
the name of the Lord. Not all, however, were
thus kindly disposed. Many feared his uncompromising sternness, as he had been represented
to them in no favorable light. He went at
once to a meeting of the Chapter, where he received the following instructions : " You will
use your utmost diligence in collecting the
revenues of the chapter, not overlooking the
smallest item. You will exhort the faithful, both
from the pulpit and from the confessional, to pay
all dues and tithes, and to testify, by their offerings, the love which they bear to the church.
You will be careful to increase the amount that
arises from the visitation of the sick, from
masses, and in general from all ecclesiastical or-
dinances. As to the administration of the sacraments, preaching, personally watching over
the flock, these are all among the duties of the
priest. But for the performance of these you
may employ a vicar to act in your stead, especially in preaching. You are to administer the
sacraments only to persons of distinction, and

when especially called upon. You are not allowed to administer them indiscriminately to people of all ranks."

We may well imagine, from our previous acquaintance with this man, who was reared among God's grandest works in nature, and who has now been made free from the servile bondage of the Romish priesthood, and brought into "the glorious liberty of the children of God," through Christ, that he will not be bound to a mere office of getting money from the people. His nature was totally averse to such employment. His spirit was too noble, too free, too generous to allow himself to be made a mere collector of revenues, as were the sordid priests of the age. Besides, he was a minister of God's word. He felt the force of that utterance of St. Paul: "Woe is me if I preach not the Gospel." We will see how he will reply to this wonderful challenge with which he is confronted upon his first entrance into Zurich.

Zwingli, with that grace which made him a distinguished man wherever he came, at first courteously tendered his thanks for the honor of his election to the vacant office. He then gave them plainly to understand that it was his firm and decided intention to preach the history of

Jesus Christ, our Redeemer, according to the
Gospel of Matthew, that the people might not,
as hitherto, to the great dishonor of the name of
God, and Him after whom they are called, know
Christ by name only, while they were ignorant
of the whole history of His life and redemption.
He would, therefore, take up the whole of the
Gospel of Matthew, and preach it, verse by
verse, and chapter by chapter without regard to
the commentaries of men, by which he would
not be bound, but give the sense according to
the light received in answer to prayer, and by a
diligent study of the originals. This he would
do to the praise and glory of God and His only
Son, for the salvation of souls and their upbuild-
ing in the true faith.

This was indeed a noble position, and canons
Utinger, Englehard, Walder and others rejoiced
at it, but Provost Frey and the canon Hoffman
were excited with alarm and grief. All felt
themselves on the eve of great events. Hoffman arose and said that he hoped the election
they had made would be followed by no bad results. Such an exposition of the Scriptures
would, in his opinion, do more harm than good,
and others warned the new priest against inno-
vations which could result in nothing but evil.
And here the matter rested for the time.

ZURICH.

CHAPTER XI.

A NEW STYLE OF PREACHING.

THE visitor to Zurich is everywhere impressed with the air of antiquity which spreads itself over the place, while at the same time he notes the thrift and enterprise which mark its modern aspect. It contains over twenty-one thousand inhabitants, and is the most flourishing Swiss town in its silk and cotton manufactories, and other industries, while at the same time it is the literary centre of Swiss-Germany. The literary activity dates from the time of Zwingli, who is still regarded as the great man of early Swiss history, as Luther is regarded in Germany. Relics of Zwingli have been carefully preserved and are shown to the modern visitor with great courtesy, as well as honest pride, by its worthy citizens.

Close beside the Limmat, which divides the city into two parts, stands the building now used as the Town library though it was called the

"Water Church" formerly, because it was surrounded by the current of the river. Here one is shown a letter which Zwingli wrote to his wife, his Greek New Testament, written out with his own hand, and many other mementoes of his life and works. Only a few steps away, resting on a terrace against the slope, stands the Cathedral, or "Minster," as it is called, where Zwingli preached. The building fronts the north, and hence has its side toward the river, which is only a few rods distant, while in its rear stands the old structure, once used as a cloister, but since the Reformation as a school, now occupied by the public school, and swarming with children and youth. It was in this building that Myconius taught, who had been so efficient in securing the post of honor for Zwingli.

The old Cathedral looks majestic and venerable as it towers above the surrounding structures, with its round-topped towers at either corner, and its broad doors opening on the terrace below. Within, it is massive in its style of architecture, but very plain. The pulpit stands at the side, against one of the heavy columns, just at the entrance to the choir, which is now stripped of every vestige of ornamentation, and is seated with pews, as is the rest of the church. Deep galleries run along either side, adding to the great capacity of the structure, but giving it a heavy and rather sombre look. The place probably wears essentially the same appearance that it did in the time of Zwingli, after the images had been removed, excepting the changes which the passing years have wrought upon its ancient, gray walls.

In this building Zwingli first made his appearance on his thirty-sixth birthday, January 1st, 1519. The church was filled by a numerous assembly, attracted by the reputation of the preacher and the desire to hear the new Gospel of which he was the acknowledged exponent. Without a lengthy and ornate introduction, but as if weightier matters engaged his thought, the preacher said : " It is to Christ that I wish to guide you,—to Christ, the true spring of salvation. This divine Word is the only food that I seek to minister to your hearts and souls." He then repeated his resolution, which he had already expressed to the canons, that he intended to expound the Gospel of Matthew, in connection with other passages of Scripture, commencing on the morrow, which would be the Christian Sabbath.

His external appearance made a fine impres-

sion. For, according to Bullinger, he was a
fine-looking man in form and figure, and he was
now in the flower of his manhood. "Let one,"
says Hagenbach, "only look at his portrait; let
him observe this energetic, well-compacted
head, this marked physiognomy, as if stone-
carved, this expansive forehead, this full, clear eye,
this compressed mouth, with the well-rounded
lips." Lavater reads in this cast of countenance
"earnestness, reflection, manly resolution, con-
centrated energy, a far-seeing, penetrating understanding." Christoffel adds: "To a powerful frame of body he added a well-modulated,
deep-toned voice. In preaching he had an
agreeable delivery, highly appropriate to the
subject. His language was simple, popular and
dignified; in exposition it was clear and per-
spicuous, in administering discipline serious and
fatherly, in warning urgent, coming home to the
soul, in comforting, warm and affectionate.

On the following day the preacher again appeared, and, agreeably to his promise, took up
the first chapter of St. Matthew's Gospel. A
still larger assemblage was present. The nave
of the "Minster," the aisles, the capacious galleries were all filled to their utmost capacity,
and every eye was fixed upon the man who was

to begin a new work in their midst. The preacher opened the Gospel, the book that had so long been sealed, and read the first page. This long catalogue of names became as a portrait gallery under the skilful tongue of the speaker. The patriarchs, the prophets, the line of human ancestry leading up to Christ, all passed in review before the delighted audience, and when the service was concluded all exclaimed in astonishment and delight: "We never heard the like of this before." It was a noted occasion, and many hopes were indulged that a great work would be wrought in Zurich, by the ministry thus auspiciously begun.

As time passed on the impression was deepened. The preacher continued his explanation of the Gospel, and, prepared by faithful study and earnest prayer, he went on to apply it to the practical affairs of life and to the deep-seated errors of the human heart. At the same time he magnified the glory and majesty of God the Father, taught that He alone was to be worshipped in spirit and in truth; and showed that all men, without distinction, could obtain salvation in none other but in Christ. At the same time he warned against every kind of superstition, of will-worship and hypocrisy. With up-

lifted voice he preached repentance and amend-
ment of life, the exercise of Christian charity
and fidelity. He attacked with resolution the
vices most spread among the people ; he preached
earnestly against inordinate expense in eating
and drinking, and the wearing of fine clothes;
against oppression of the poor, against mercenary wars, and the taking of gifts or bribes in
the shape of pensions. Herein he spared neither
pope nor emperor, king nor duke, princes nor
nobles, not even the confederates themselves.

All his discourses rested on the foundation of
God's Word, which he explained and expounded
as he went along, and it was pervaded by the
conviction that, in the end, and by the help of
God, truth and righteousness would gain the
day over lying, error, hypocrisy and vice. This
description comes from his contemporaries, one
of whom adds: " All his comfort was in God,
in whom he trusted, and in whom he rejoiced.
He exhorted the town of Zurich to place their
trust in Him."

That Zwingli was a stern and gloomy prophet, who never presented the consolations of
the Gospel, who never dwelt upon the love and
tenderness of Christ, is a great mistake. Fear-
less as he was in attacking vice in every form,

he always had regard to the intellectual and spiritual deficiencies of his hearers. He once said of his own course: "Christ praises, very highly, the faithful steward who gave to the household of his Lord their meat in due season. Matt. 24: 45. I strive to set before me the duty of dividing the word of God so that there may be the greater fruits. We do not plow and sow in winter, but in spring. So I sought to adapt my words to the condition of my hearers, giving each his portion of meat in due season. I pointed them to the mercy of God revealed in Jesus Christ. Thus I fed them with milk, for they were not able to receive the strong meat of the word, till some of them who were most bitter against me, at first, in the end, gave themselves to the Lord."

The fact alluded to here is only what we might expect from the earnest, eloquent, and tender manner in which Zwingli preached. One year after he began his ministry here, it is said, two thousand persons had given their hearts to God. He himself adds: "They felt in their hearts how sweet the Lord is, and that every one who knows Him aright must cry out with the disciples, 'Lord to whom shall we go? Thou hast the words of eternal life.' Or as in

the words of Solomon, " I held him and would
not let him go." For he who has learned to
know God aright, and has been led home by His
hand, like a strayed child, can never leave Him;
and though by the force of bodily pains the
mouth were brought to deny him, yet the heart
would still adhere to him, for it knows that God
alone is its salvation through Jesus Christ.
And I tell those this day who preach the word
of God, and who preach it so as to draw salvation from it alone, that the trust in the one
living and true God will go on to increase while
the trust in the refuges of lies will decrease and
decay ; and since man must put his whole confidence in God, and in Him alone, I had rather
yield somewhat to human weakness than that
the doctrine of Christ were altogether put
aside." Here we see the ripest Christian experience portrayed, blended with tender pity for
the errors of the weak and ignorant.

Christoffel remarks the admirable union in
Zwingli of heroic courage and firm resolution,
with a tender delicacy of feeling toward the
weak. The man who was so firmly founded in
the word of God that he could say : " I am sure
that this is the mind of God ; and though you
threaten me with all the malice of Rome, with

all the fire of Aetna, or of hell itself, I shall not
budge from it," could yet admit to a boy who recalled to his mind a false expression he had
made use of in the pulpit, that he was wrong,
saying to the critical youngster, " We can learn
much from boys when they are sharp and atten-
tive." In this manner Zwingli soon won the
love of many hearts, and his influence over them
was always salutary, for he brought to them
not only fresh instruction, but he led them to
the feet of the Saviour, and there they found
rest to their souls.

At the hearing of his first sermon there were
men who before this had entirely withdrawn
themselves from all religious service, on the
ground that the sermons delivered there lacked
the one thing needful, which the preacher had
not himself learned—the truth. These men said :
" God be praised, here is a preacher of the
truth indeed ; he will be our Moses, and will
lead us out of Egypt." Myconius, as usual, is
quite carried away by his friend's eloquence,
and says : "Never had there been seen a priest
in the pulpit with such an imposing appearance
and commanding power, so that you were irre-
sistibly led to believe that a man from the apostolic times was standing before you."

The fact that such a distinguished preacher was at the Minster drew vast crowds to hear the word of God. And as many farmers attended the market on Fridays who were unable to attend on Sunday, Zwingli preached on that day from the Psalms, as he continued to do from the Gospels on Sunday. These discourses had a marked effect upon these people from the surrounding districts; and many of them carried the seeds of divine truth back with them to their distant homes. This led the Town Council of Zurich to issue a mandate to the parish priests, curates and others, in town and country: "That they should freely and everywhere preach the Holy Gospels and the Epistles, and that they all should speak the same language, as the Spirit of God should direct them, and they were only to teach that which they could prove from the Bible. But as for the doctrines and commandments that were of man's institution, they should let them alone." It was due to this fact, no doubt, that many of the more earnest and worthy priests of the canton came into accord with Zwingli, and, imbibing his spirit, began to preach Bible truth.

But along with this pleasant picture we must present the fact that many opponents

were to be found on every side, and besides
grave troubles afflicted the affairs of government
in the Cantons, in which it was the duty of Zwingli, as "Folk-Preacher," to take part. He was
constantly found among the people, visiting and
conversing with them freely everywhere, trying
to follow the example of the Divine Master, of
whom it was said: "The common people heard
him gladly, and He went about doing good."

The sociability of Zwingli contributed not a
little to his popularity. He frequented the
places where the civic companies or trading
bodies held their meetings, explaining to the
people the leading articles of the Christian faith,
or holding familiar conversation with them.
He treated all with equal respect, and it was
charged against him by his enemies that "He
invited the country folks to dinner, walked with
them, talked to them about God, and often put
the evil one in their hearts and his own writings into their pockets."

He still loved music, but indulged in it with
moderation, notwithstanding which his enemies
named him the "Evangelical lute-player and
piper." Faber, who was formerly his friend,
reproved him for his love of music. He replied:
"My dear Faber, thou knowest not what music

is. I do not deny that I have learned to play the lute and violin, and other instruments, and at worst they serve me to quiet little children when they cry; but as for thee thou art too holy for music; and dost thou not know, then, that David was a cunning player on the harp, and how he chased the evil spirit out of Saul? Oh! if thy ears were but awake to the notes of the celestial lute, the evil spirit of ambition and greediness of wealth, by which thou art possessed, would in like manner depart from thee." The Reformer composed the music of several of his Christian lyrics, and it is to be hoped that some one will discover and publish these manuscripts as a contribution to our reformation history, in which field there is abundant material which will richly repay the successful collector.

It belongs to this part of our work to speak of Zwingli's system of labor, also. From sunrise till ten o'clock he employed himself in reading, writing, or translating; the Hebrew especially during that portion of the day occupied much of his attention. After dinner he gave audience to those who had any communication to make to him, or stood in need of any of his advice; he walked out in company with his friends and visited his people. At two o'clock he resumed his walk. He took a short turn after supper and then began writing letters, which often engaged him until midnight. He always read and wrote standing, and never allowed the customary allotment of his time to be disturbed, except for some very important cause.

In all this we can plainly see how well Zwingli was adapted to be the forerunner of the Protestant pastor, how nearly he hit upon the spirit, life, and conduct of the minister of a free Gospel, going out and in among his people, not clad in priestly robes, and bearing himself with a lofty ecclesiastical dignity, but as one of their own number, like them responsible to God for his conduct, he led the way toward heaven. He was also remarkably cheerful in spirit. No calamity at this time ever daunted him. His speech was ever hopeful, his heart ever steadfast. He sat alternately at the poor man's scanty board, and the banquet table of the great, as his Master had done before him, and everywhere he strove to advance the cause of Christ.

9

CHAPTER XII.

SHADOWS AND SORROWS.

WHEN the warm days of July and August approach, and the melting snow and ice swell the streams which pour down the ravines of the Alps, great clouds of vapor often arise and hide their lofty summits from the sight. These clouds are wafted onward by the summer breeze, and cast their shadows upon the long grassy slopes which lie between the mountains and the lakes. Their dusky forms may stand for those shadows which are now to fall upon the eventful experience of Zwingli.

First among the troubles which came upon him at this time was the approach of the monk Samson, from whom we lately parted at Bremgarten, towards Zurich. Partial success in his sale of indulgences had made him bold, and in his controversy with Dean Bullinger he had resolved to appeal to the deputies of the Confederation at Zurich for permission to continue his trade throughout the cantons. Both parties came on to test the issue before the deputies; and as Zwingli saw the gradual progress of the bold monk, he again lifted up his voice against the whole system by which Samson was getting great gains. The latter when on his road to Zurich said: " I know that Zwingli will speak against me, but I will stop his mouth."

Zwingli knew well the blessedness of the sense of sins forgiven, but he knew also that only Christ could forgive them. He said: " When Satan attempts to terrify me, crying aloud: ' Lo! this and that thou hast left undone, though God has commanded it!'—the gentle voice of the Gospel brings me instant comfort, for it whispers : ' What thou canst not do, and of a truth thou canst do nothing, that Christ does for thee, and does it thoroughly.' ' Yes, when my heart is wrung with anguish by reason of my impotency, and the weakness of the flesh, my spirit revives at the sound of these joyful words ; Christ is thy sinlessness ! Christ is thy righteousness ! Christ is the Alpha and the Omega ; Christ is the beginning and the end ; Christ is all; He can do all ! All created things will disappoint and deceive thee ; but Christ, the sinless and the righteous, will accept thee.'"

Referring again to Samson, he said: "No man has power to remit sins—except Christ alone, who is very God and very man in one. Go if thou wilt, and buy indulgences. But be assured, that thou art in nowise absolved. They who sell the remission of sin for money, are but companions of Simon the magician, the friends of Balaam, the ambassador of Satan." When Samson at last with the effrontery of his craft arrived at an inn in the suburbs of Zurich, and while he had his foot in the stirrup ready to mount his horse and ride into the city, he was accosted by messengers from the council, who while courteous as they thought becoming towards an agent of the Pope, intimated to him that he might forego his intention of appearing in Zurich. The seller of pardons replied: "I have somewhat to communicate to the Diet, in the name of his Holiness.

This, Daubigne says, was only a stratagem. It was determined, however, that he should be admitted; but as he spoke of nothing but his bulls, he was dismissed, after having been forced to withdraw the excommunication he had pronounced against the Dean of Bremgarten. He departed in high-dudgeon; and soon after, the Pope recalled him to Italy. A cart, drawn by

three horses, and loaded with coin, obtained under false pretences from the poor, rolled before
him over those steep roads of the St. Gottard,
along which he had passed eight months before,
indigent, unattended, and encumbered by no
burden save his papers."

But a far greater conflict awaited Zwingli
than this in connection with his patriotic efforts.
It has been remarked already that, even when at
Glarus, he had taken strong grounds against the
foreign military service, which had been so
long the bane of Switzerland. As the evil continued he could not be silent, and perform his duty
to his people. And it was the more necessary
for him to take a deep interest, and an active
part in the affairs of state, since in Switzerland
the Government was in the hands of the people.

"No nation," says Seebohm, "was so ab-
solutely without a central authority as the
Swiss. Each canton was as independent of the
others, for most purposes, as the petty feudal
states of Germany. When Machiavelli complained of the divisions of Italy preventing its
becoming a nation, he warned the Italians of the
danger of a country being 'cantonized' like
Switzerland. But there was this difference between a Swiss canton and a petty feudal state.

In the Swiss canton there was no feudal lord; the people governed themselves. It was not a feudal lordship, but a little republic of communes or villages of the primitive Teutonic type, in which the civil power was vested in the community. If therefore in a Swiss canton the civil power took to itself the ecclesiastical power hitherto held by the Pope, that power vested in the people, not, as in other countries, in the prince or king."

The political troubles of the Swiss were renewed in 1520 and still more in 1521, by the intrigues of the Pope, and by the efforts of Francis I., king of France, and the emperor Charles V., to secure their aid in the wars which these rival princes waged against one another. Francis finally succeeded, in a Diet of the confederates held at Lucerne, on the third of May, 1521, in concluding a treaty of alliance with all the cantons except Zurich. Zwingli was now active, as he had need to be, to prevent his people from engaging in this unseemly strife. He said : " Next to my concern for the word of God, the interests of the Confederacy lie nearest my heart. For the longing desire of my heart, and the great object of my teaching, has been the preservation of the Confederacy, that it might remain, as handed down to us from our fathers, true to itself, and free from service under foreign masters, and that the members of it might live together in peace and friendship."

Zwingli lifted up his voice energetically against this evil of foreign service. " Our fathers," said he, " conquered their enemies, and won their freedom, relying on no other arm but the arm of the Almighty, and they were ready at all times to recognize His intervention in their behalf." This he could say with confidence, for the Swiss, in ancient times began their battles with prayer, and when they gained a victory, they fell on their knees, and thanked God for His help. The preacher then pointed out the dangers that would come to them again from engaging in foreign service. They would be in danger of God's judgments; their laws would be trampled upon; idleness would again characterize the returned soldiers; selfishness would be paramount, and strife among brethren would be sure to follow. In consequence of these wise counsels Zurich resolved to observe a strict neutrality, and to adhere to the treaty of perpetual peace made between all the cantons in 1516.

Nevertheless some three thousand soldiers enlisted under the influence of the Pope, professedly

to protect the territory of the church, but really
to fight for Charles V. When the troops were
well on their way to Italy the secret of their
destination leaked out, and an express was
sent to recall them, but on condition that they
were not to be employed against the French,
they were allowed to proceed. The united
forces of the Pope and the Emperor triumphed
over those of France; and the Swiss returned
without either laurels or booty. The greatest
dissatisfaction now was cherished by the other
cantons towards Zurich; and Zwingli, who had
strenuously resisted the whole movement, was
blamed most of all. He was never forgiven by
the other cantons, and their enmity was not sa-
tiated even with his death.

Zwingli had enfeebled his health by over-
work, and made a journey eastward to the celebrated baths of Pfaffers, about this time, that he
might rest and receive the benefit of the water
of the hot springs. The place was not calculated to cheer the spirit of the reformer, whatever the water might do for his health. The baths
were situated in the frightful gorge formed
by the impetuous torrent of the Tamina.
Daniel, the hermit, named it the " infernal
gulf;" and well he might, for the limestone cliffs

are from 500 to 800 feet in height, while the gorge is only from 30 to 50 feet wide, through which rushes the roaring waters of the river. It is said that the bath-house, now located in the gorge, enjoys sunshine in the height of summer from 10 till 4 o'clock, but in the building where Zwingli lodged it was necessary to burn torches at midday. This was the ancient seat of a monastery, and many were the stories told of fearful spectres which might be seen there gliding to and fro amidst the darkness. This gloom is mentioned by many writers as a preparation of Zwingli for coming trouble.

Trouble soon came in the form of news that the plague had broken out in Zurich. Zwingli hastened to return that he might perform a pastor's part in this trying emergency. The " Great Death," as it was called, swept on from the east over the deep chasm of Tamina, where Zwingli was, and, as a great shadow of destruction, fell upon nearly all the towns and villages of Switzerland, late in the summer of 1519. During the time of its frightful ravages it swept away no fewer than 2,500 souls in Zurich. After sending away a number of young men who were students in his house, among whom was his brother Andrew, Zwingli began his faithful work among the sick and dying of his flock. As he went forward with his duties many watched him with admiration, but with solicitude as well, for they knew not what moment the fell destroyer might lay him low.

A friend in Basel, Conrad Brunner, wrote: "I rejoice greatly that thou standest untouched and unharmed by the arrows of death which are flying around. But my joy will not be free of anxiety so long as thou daily exposest thyself to great peril by visiting the sick of the plague. Forget not, while bringing consolation to others, to take care of thine own life." With heroic courage he visited the sick and the dying without intermission, and supplied them with the rich consolations of the Gospel. In his sermons he raised the sinking hearts of his terrified congregation with the promises of the word of life, and pointed them to Christ, who quickens the weary and heavy ladened. Many among his people also trembled for the life of their faithful pastor, as they saw him moving about amidst the thickly-flying darts of death, himself bearing around the cup of salvation.

The anxiety of friends was but too well founded, for at the end of September he was also smitten with the pestilence. The grief of his people was great when they realized that their pastor was stretched upon a bed of sickness, perhaps of death. Friends of evangelic truth at a distance were also deeply moved at the tidings. Dr. Hedio wrote to him: " We were deeply afflicted when we heard that this murderous disease had seized you also, for who would not grieve if the deliverer of his country, if the trumpet of the Gospel, if the courageous herald of the truth should be stricken down in the prime of life, high in hope, and in the midst of his usefulness." The feelings of his own soul during his sickness the Reformer poured forth in the following hymn, of which we furnish a new version as nearly as possible in the meters and language of the original German:

> Lord, hear my anxious pleading,
> O, help me in this strait;
> Upon my door is knocking,
> The doleful hand of death.
> Thou, Lord, for him in conflict
> The might of mercy hast;
> Stay, Christ, O! stay beside me,
> And help me to the last.
>
> My Father, if it be Thy will,
> O grant me saving grace,
> And make this cup pass from me,
> Nor hide me from Thy face.

Send comfort to my spirit,
E'en while my pains increase;
This is my hour of anguish,
From tossings no release.

Thou art, O Lord, my Maker,
And I Thy creature am,
As clay in hand of potter
I'm fashioned by Thy hand.
At length in holy stillness
My soul with Thee shall rest,
Thy will shall be my pleasure
Be it in life or death.

The disease gained ground. His friends in deep affliction beheld the man on whom the hopes of Switzerland and the church reposed, ready to be swallowed up by the grave. His bodily powers and natural faculties were forsaking him. His heart was smitten with dismay, yet he found strength sufficient left him to turn to God and to cry:

Hear, O my God, 'tis Thee I seek,
My malady increases;
The sharpness of my pain exceeds,
My heart is pierced with grieving.
To Thee, my Comforter, I flee,
Haste, Lord, to help and strengthen me,
Bring comfort, blessed Jesus.

Yes, Saviour, from Thy presence sweet
Comes help to them that trust Thee;
In faith they clasp Thy pierced feet
And joyful rest upon Thee;
On Thee, for aye, their hope is set,
Their treasure Thou, they ne'er forget
When earthly good doth perish.

Surely I see with griping hand
The evil One approaching,
And him, though weak, I must withstand,
He shall not thus o'erthrow me.
For while my faith is strong and fast
Thou, Lord, wilt make my courage last,
By fear of hell unshaken.

Great was the consternation that prevailed throughout the city. The friends of the papacy thought that it would be dreadful if he were not reconciled with Rome, but no one seems to have disturbed him with this subject. The believers cried to God night and day, earnestly entreating that He would restore their faithful pastor. The alarm had spread from Zurich to the mountains of Toggenburg. Even there the plague had been ravaging. Seven or eight persons had fallen a prey to it in Wildhaus, one of them a servant of Zwingli's brother Nicholas. No tidings were received from the Reformer. His brother Andrew wrote: " Let me know

what is thy state, my beloved brother. The
Abbot and all our brothers salute thee." It
would seem that Zwingli's parents were already
dead, since they are not mentioned here. But
that glimmering spark of life, which had been
left unquenched, began now to burn more
brightly. Though laboring still under great
bodily weakness his soul was filled with a
deep impression that God had called him to re-
place the candle of his word on the deserted
candlestick of his church. The plague had re-
linquished its victim. With strong emotion
Zwingli now exclaimed:

Restored, through Thy great mercy,
My God, I'm well again ;
My joyful lips do praise Thee,
I sing in gladsome strain.
Since Thou hast been my Helper,
And life Thou didst restore,
My soul shall ever bless Thee
And, daily, more and more.

Had death securely bound me,
I would from earth be free,
And even now be standing,
My blessed Lord, by Thee.
Now must I bide my summons
And wait for death again,
Prepared for work or suffering,
Prepared for greater pain.

Yet, since Thou thus hast willed it,
I joyful journey on,
With true and willing spirit,
Till pilgrimage is done.
Through pain and strife I'm pressing,
To Thee, O Lord, I come—
To yonder blissful haven,
To my eternal home.

CHAPTER XIII.

BRAVE EFFORTS FOR REFORM.

THE Cathedral Church of Zurich, known by the name of 'the Minster,' was a very ancient and well-endowed institution. When Zwingli became its pastor, in 1519, its council consisted of twenty-four canons, to whom were added a number of chaplains. All these in former times lived upon the revenues of the foundation, but performed no other service than to sing in the choir during canonical hours. The whole labor of preaching and of the care of souls was left to the one pastor, called people's priest, and his two assistants. The burden of this great charge lay upon Zwingli, and earnestly did he labor to fulfil his duty.

When the Reformer arose from his sick bed, snatched as it were from the very jaws of death, he manifested even greater zeal than before. Notwithstanding the fact that his enemies continued on his track, he won the affec-

tions of the people to such a degree that in 1521
he was elected to canonship by the chapter.
He might now, agreeably to the old custom,
have retired from active life and passed the re-
mainder of his days in dignified leisure; but he
retained his pastorship, and continued to perform all its duties, as before, though his seat in
the council gave him a voice and vote in its de-
liberations, and more freedom in his work.

For a time, in connection with his other
duties, he pursued the study of the Hebrew
language, under an able teacher, and as before
in the case of the Greek, he soon made rapid
progress. He was thus enabled to read the
Old Testament in the original. A deeper seri-
ousness now manifested itself in the spirit of the
Reformer, due no doubt to his late sickness, but
more especially to the need that he discerned
for reformation in the church. He was hardly
yet fully recovered, for in November he wrote:
"The sickness has enfeebled my memory and
prostrated my spirits. I often in preaching
loose the thread of my discourse. My whole
frame is oppressed with languor, and I am little
better than a dead man." But he soon rose to
strength again, and though 'faint was still pur-
suing.'

10

There were three monasteries in Zurich, and as Zwingli, and those who stood with him affirmed that the pure word of God should only be proclaimed to the people, the monks in these monasteries fearing that their calling might be overthrown, petitioned the council to forbid any one to preach against their customs, on the ground that it would disturb the community. The council granted their petition, and a violent contest followed in the pulpits between the Reformers and the monks. The council referred the matter to a committee, and after a stormy debate the presiding officer exhorted them not to preach anything that might cause disturbance.

Zwingli solemnly declared: "I cannot accept this command. I will preach the Gospel free and without limitation, as was formerly resolved upon. I am bishop and parson of Zurich. To me the care of souls is entrusted. I, not the monks, have taken the oath. They must yield and not I. If they preach lies I will come up to the very pulpit of their cloisters and contradict them. I, for my part, if I preach anything contrary to the Holy Gospel am willing to subject myself to the censure of the chapter, nay, of every citizen, and let myself be punished for it." This bold stand decided the council, and they granted to Zwingli and his friends permission to preach in the chapels of the convents. Truth had thus again conquered.

Soon after this an event occurred which gave the enemies of reform an opportunity to attack Zwingli. Early in 1522 he stated in a sermon that feasts appointed by the church, in which certain meats were forbidden to be eaten at certain times, a release from which could only be obtained by donations to the church, had no foundation in the word of God, but were directly contrary to it. He said: "Many think that to eat flesh is improper, nay a sin, although God has nowhere forbidden it, but to sell human flesh in slaughter and carnage they hold to be no sin at all." Reports of this sermon were carried by the monks to the Bishop of Constance, who sent a delegation to Zurich on April 7th, 1522, who set themselves to gain a secret meeting of the authorities and have Zwingli condemned. Though they tried to prevent it, the council decided that the pastor should be present at the conference. The bishop's ambassadors were very smooth and polite in speech, while they hinted that contentious and dangerous men taught that human institutions and rites are no more to be regarded, and this

would undermine the church. Zwingli replied
that Zurich was more peaceable than any other
town in the confederacy. He added: " For my
part, one may fast the whole year, if he have not
enough in the forty days; only I hold that
fasts should not be imposed on any one by the
threat of excommunication, but that every one
should be left to use his own liberty in the matter." The mission returned, having entirely
failed in its object.

On May second the bishop sent to all the
clergy a warning against the new views, without naming Zwingli, but covertly striking at
him. The Reformer availed himself of a pamphlet published at Bern and directed against the
bishop, which he circulated through the community. On May 24th the bishop made a third
attack by a letter prepared by his vicar Fabel,
and directed to the council at Zurich warning
them against the poison of new teachers. Zwingli answered this in a pamphlet of his own, entitled " The Beginning and the End," so named
because he wished it to be final on the subject
on his part. He spoke respectfully of the
bishop, but ascribed his course to evil advisers,
whom he advises him to dismiss, and, continuing, answers the letter sentence by sentence.

Matters now began to assume a serious aspect. A Diet was assembled at Lucerne in May, at the instance of the bishop, for the purpose of applying stringent measures. A complaint was at once lodged against the adherents of the new doctrine and the preacher of Zurich. A motion was immediately passed : " In the name of the confederacy to instruct the priests, whose sermons produce disunion and disturbance among the people, to desist from such preaching." Sorely as this action annoyed Zwingli he did not allow himself to be discouraged by it, or to relax his zeal for the cause of Christ. He heard in the brewing storm a call to uphold the sacred banner of the truth.

Accordingly he called together at Einsiedeln a number of the evangelical clergy in the month of June, 1522, and laid before them two petitions for their signatures, one in German to the Diet, the other in Latin to the Bishop of Constance. The petitions were different in form, but in substance the same, and prayed : " That the preaching of the Gospel might not be forbidden, and that it might be permitted to the priests to marry." " Little as was the influence," says Christoffel, " which this petition exerted on those to whom it was addressed, it still produced great effects among the lower orders of clergy and the people. It became a banner around which the friends of divine truth and of the rights of conscience leagued in one covenant, that disappointed all the schemes of combined iniquity. On the fifteenth of August of this year the chapter of the canton of Zurich which comprised the clergy from the sources of the Linth to the junction of the Limmat with the Reuss, met and made the great spiritual movement of the times a chief topic of debate. By Zwingli's influence this assembly unanimously adopted the following resolution: "To preach nothing but what is contained in the Word of God." From this time on his watchword was: "We must obey God rather than man."

The resolution passed at Einsiedeln relating to the marriage of the priests, and which was forwarded with the petition to the bishop and the Diet, prepares the way to speak of Zwingli's marriage. This event has a great deal of romance surrounding it, as well as danger. It is generally dated on April 12, 1524, though supposed by some to have taken place at an earlier period, but not published on account of the troublous nature of the times, which rendered the marriage of a priest a cause of stumbling and offence to many.

Zwingli became acquainted with Anna Reinhardt through his interest in her son, Gerold Meyer, who came to his study in Zurich upon some errand during 1521. Zwingli appears to have formed a strong attachment to this youth, and by a sort of natural consequence became attracted to the excellent qualities of the mother. She had married young, above her station in life, to John Meyer von Knonau, a young nobleman in the neighborhood of Zurich, where his father's castle was situated. The elder Meyer was highly incensed when he heard of his son's marriage to Anna, and disinherited him. After a few years of wedded life Anna's husband was removed from her by death. Thus in the year 1513 she was left a widow with the care of three children, one son and two daughters. She thought only of the education of her children, for which purpose no means were at hand.

The grandfather was inexorable, seeming to have no interest whatever in his destitute grandchildren, until one day he happened to be near the fish-market in Zurich, when he saw little Gerold at play. The beauty of the child attracted his attention, and he inquired whose boy it was. Upon being told that it was his

son's he was moved to deep feeling. He
brought the widow and her children to his
wealthy home and rejoiced in their companion-
ship

The pastor of Zurich, now convinced that the
Scriptures nowhere forbid the marriage of
Christian ministers, but on the other hand en-
courage this ordinance that the minister may be
the head of a Christian household, sought the
hand of the young widow and they were joined
in marriage. She proved to be in every way
worthy of his choice, but she had great sorrows
to bear in after time, even greater than those
she had experienced in her earlier years.

Their family consisted of four children : The
eldest daughter, Regula married Zwingli's successor, Ralph Gwalter, and died in 1565. The
youngest daughter, Anna, died early. William,
the eldest son, died in 1541, while a student of
theology at Strassburg ; and Ulric, the younger
son, became afterward, a professor of theology
at Zurich. With him the male line of the Reformer became extinct.

CHAPTER XIV.

DANGER AND DEFENCE.

ALL thoughtful men knew that a grave issue was at hand, when the year 1523 dawned upon the reformation in Switzerland. The Diet which was composed of the delegates from the various cantons opposed to the reforms introduced by Zwingli in Zurich had met in Lucerne the May previous, and sent forth an ominous warning, which was followed by threat after threat, from the same quarter. Even as dark clouds roll athwart the sky, and gleams of lightning flash out from the storm-center, while as yet it is far distant from the spectator; so Zwingli saw the front of the coming tempest, and knew that every shaft of death was pointed at his heart. But while he knew all this, only too well, his conscience would not suffer him to relax his efforts for needed reformation.

In the month of August previous, all the pastors in Zurich had given up their pensions.

During the same month a convention had been held at Rapperschwyl, in which 38 parishes were represented, and all these proposed to stand together in defence of the truth. These pastors resolved unanimously to preach only what they could prove by the word of God. One of them, pastor Weiss, was soon afterward imprisoned at Constance, for rejecting the invocation of the Virgin Mary, and for refusing longer to obey the rule of celibacy. He escaped with his life, but other pious men were less favored.

There was a strong desire on the part of many godly persons, expressed at this time, for the removal of all images from their churches. Zwingli was favorable to this change, but he exhorted to patience, and delay, until there was a stronger public sentiment to sustain the movement. But a citizen of Stadelhofen, named Hottinger, rebuked the miller of that place for keeping a cross with the image of the Saviour upon it beside the highway, where many persons paid it reverence. The miller replied : " If you are empowered to remove it, I leave you to do so." Hottinger construed this as permission, and proceeded, with others, to take the image down. Great excitement followed ; the parti-

sans of Rome clamored for his blood, and the
men were arrested. Zwingli took the ground
that they had not committed sin against God by
this act. But that they should be justly punished for having resorted to violence without
the sanction of the magistrate. Hottinger was
set at liberty, but he was afterward arrested at
Baden, brought before the Diet in Lucerne in
March 1524, condemned to death, and beheaded.
His last words were: "Into Thy hands I com-
mend my soul, O! my Lord and Redeemer,
Jesus Christ! Have mercy on me and receive
me unto Thyself." Thus died Nicholas Hottinger, the first martyr of the Reformed Church.

The feeling in favor of abolishing the images
kept increasing however, and one day a pastor
of St. Peter's Church in Zurich observing a
number of poor people before the church door
said to one of his colleagues: "I should like to
strip those wooden idols, and clothe those poor
members of Jesus Christ." A few days after, at
three o'clock in the morning, the saints and their
fine trappings were missing. The council sent
the pastor to prison, although he protested that he
had no hand in removing them. Threats were
now multiplied on the part of the papal cantons
against Zurich, and fierce controversies followed.

The magistrates undecided as to the course
they ought to pursue, sent word to the bishops
of Constance, Basel and Coira, to despatch a
joint commission to Zurich. But it was the
policy of these bishops to keep silent for the
present, and the deputies did not appear. The
council assembled, and canon Hoffman stepped
forward to defend the Pope, and denied that the
body had power to take action in the case.
Zwingli claimed that the council could regulate
matters of worship within its territory, and
said: "Hong and Kussnacht, two villages in
the neighborhood of Zurich, are more of a church
than all the bishops and popes put together."
Thus, says Daubigne, "did Zwingli assert the
rights of Christians in general, whom Rome had
stript of their inheritance. Here we see the
beginnings of the Presbyterian system. He
was engaged in delivering Zurich from the juris-
diction of the bishops of Constance—he was
likewise detaching it from the hierarchy of
Rome; and on this thought of the flock, and
the assembly of believers, he was laying the
foundation of a new church order to which other
countries would afterwards adhere."

At this time also the question of the mass
was violently agitated. Zwingli had taught

from the pulpit that the customs of the mass were a departure from the teachings of Scripture, and from the practice of the early church. But he counselled against hasty and unauthorized action in the premises. He therefore requested that a conference be called at Zurich for the free discussion of the questions then agitating the church. Accordingly the meeting was called for January 28th, 1523, for which the Reformer prepared his celebrated 67 theses. They were ably formulated, and even yet stand as the bulwarks of protestantism. They teach that: " Jesus Christ is the only way of salvation for all who have been, are, or shall be." Christians are all the brethren of Christ, and they have no " fathers " upon earth. No compulsion in cases of conscience should be used, unless the seditious disturb the peace of others. Christ offered Himself upon the cross for our sins, therefore the mass, or Lord's Supper, is not a sacrifice, but a commemoration of a sacrifice, and a seal of the redemption He has procured for us.

On the 26th of October another conference was held in Zurich, at which over nine hundred people were present. The discussions of this body hastened the cause of reform, but the rashness of a few misguided men who, afterwards, would proceed. with great violence, was wisely restrained, or else a religious war would have been, at once, inaugurated. As it was, the images were generally removed from the churches in Zurich, in some cases it may be, with undue violence.

We who sit in safety in our free churches, are wont to criticise every extravagance which marked the work of the reformation. But we should ever remember that in all movements of this kind, fanatics will arise, who, with other indiscreet persons, will often bring reproach upon the cause which they champion, but misrepresent in spirit. Zwingli had ever to contend with this difficulty even as Luther did in Germany. He did not, at once, discard the mass for the time was not ripe for it; but he modified its celebration August 1523, and finally substituted the Lord's Supper for it in 1525.

The Anabaptists as they were called, because they rebaptized those who had been baptized in infancy, arose during the time of Zwingli and brought sore afflictions upon themselves and others. At first they baptized by sprinkling, but subsequently immersed the candidates in the rivers. In connection with this they taught that warfare should be at once begun; and many pretended to have supernatural visions, and others affirmed that they were inspired with the Holy Ghost. Great extravagances were practiced, which in some cases resulted in the loss of life; as when in Thuringia one fanatic told another that he must behead him, for the Lord had commanded it; the second obeyed and cut off the head of the one making the proposal, with a sword.

Zwingli greatly deplored all fanaticism, counselled against it, and used moderation with his firmness in removing abuses. But the papal cantons charged every thing of this kind to his account, and nursed their wrath against him, and only waited their opportunity to cut him off. As they could not attack him directly in his stronghold they fell upon his friends, in the surrounding districts, and hastened to persecute them. Pastor Oechslin, Zwingli's friend when at Ensiedeln, who was now settled at Burg, became very obnoxious to the papists. The bishop tried to expel him from his charge, but his people sustained him and refused to let him go. At last the magistrate was ordered to take him by force. He was attacked in his own house, dragged out of his bed at midnight, and hurried off to prison. The whole community was aroused; the church bell was rung in alarm, and many persons spent the night at the river's side, over which the prisoner had been carried. As a result of this outrage some misguided persons were led to take vengeance; and during the agitation a band of disorderly men took possession of a convent, when, by some means it caught fire, and was burned to the ground.

The Romanists held Diet after Diet, and at last charged four men named Rutiman, John Wirt and his two sons with the crime. The sons of Wirt were pastors, and the offence was never proved against them, and they constantly affirmed their innocence. The Romish cantons called upon Zurich to give them up; and at last, in an evil hour, and contrary to Zwingli's earnest entreaty, the four men were marched off to Baden. A farcical trial was held, and three of the men were beheaded amid scoffs and jeers.

The fire of persecution was now burning fiercely. Threats came with the report of every Diet that was held by the Romanists. Affairs were indeed desperate. And each new volley was aimed at Zwingli, who was acknowledged on all sides to be the leader of the Reformed. No wonder that at times he became discouraged. He said that he was hated and attacked because he had preached Christ, and had besought the church to abolish the abuses. All the cantons made a league against Zurich except Bern. The threats of war were about to be fulfilled; and the papal cantons fearing that they would not have force enough to cope with the brave Zurichers, made an alliance with Austria by which the latter would furnish troop and horse, if needful.

This brought on the " First war of Cappel." All the cantons were in a state of confusion, and in certain parts violence was used against the Reformed. A minister of the Gospel named James Keyser, while on his way to a preaching appointment, was seized as he was passing through a piece of forest, hurried off to the canton of Schwitz, and burned at the stake. This aroused Zwingli. The Romanists were already recruiting soldiers at Zug, ostensibly with the object of attacking Zurich. Zwingli said it was time to arise for defence. Recruiting began in Zurich; and when the men were ready to issue forth in defence of their rights, Zwingli brought out his old armor that he had worn during the campaigns in Italy, and went forth with them.

The little army of Zurich took its way over

11

the Albis, and came to a halt at Cappel, within
its own territory. The army of Zug advanced
to meet them ; and when it seemed certain that
blood must be shed, negotiations were undertaken, which resulted favorably ; and on June
26th, 1529, while the two armies confronted
each other a treaty was formed, and war was
averted. The conditions were that the Gospel
should be preached freely throughout the whole
confederacy ; that all alliances against it should
be null and void ; that the images should be left
to the choice of the people ; the five cantons
were to pay the expense of the war ; and Schwitz
should pay a thousand florins to the children of
the martyred Keyser.

The soldiers, now rejoiced, and fraternized,
ate and drank together, and said we are all
Swiss, we are brethren. Thankful that for the
present at least, war was averted, Zwingli returned to his home ; but he still had fears that
at some future time when they should be better
prepared the papal cantons would renew the
attack ; and his fears were to be sadly realized.

During the time that Zwingli was waiting for
the negotiations to cease, which were to avert
war for the time, he composed the following
hymn, setting it to music ; and in this form it

was often sung by the Swiss. We furnish the
free paraphrase of another hand, in which
form it could very well be sung in English:—

> Do Thou direct Thy chariot Lord,
>   And guide us at Thy will;
> Without Thy aid our strength is vain
>   And useless all our skill.
> Look down upon Thy saints below
> When prostrate laid beneath the foe.
>
> Beloved Pastor, who hast saved
>   Our souls from death and sin:
> Uplift Thy voice, awake Thy sheep;
>   That slumbering lie within
> Thy fold; and curb, with Thy right hand,
> The rage of Satan's furious band.
>
> Send down Thy peace and banish strife,
>   Let bitterness depart;
> Revive the spirit of Thy grace
>   In each true Christian's heart;
> Then shall Thy church forever sing
> The praises of her heavenly King.

CHAPTER XV.

WHILE peace temporarily spread her mantle over Switzerland, and the Reformed religion was unmolested at Zurich, its central seat, Zwingli was invited to meet with the great Reformer of Saxony, Martin Luther, for a comparison of their views respecting the Lord's Supper. Zwingli, anxious that every difference between the Reformers might be removed, accepted willingly the invitation of Philip, landgrave of Hesse, to meet at his castle at Marburg for a friendly conference. The council of Zurich discouraged Zwingli from attempting the journey, for fear that he would be slain; but he persevered in his resolution, and set out unattended for Basel, where he met his friend Œcolampadius, with whom he went on to Marburg.

Luther seems to have consented rather reluctantly to the invitation, having doubts as to the issue of the conference. Myconius says that

164

Zwingli and Œcolampadius misunderstood Luther from the beginning in presupposing that he held the gross view, that we eat the body of Christ just as we eat common food, a view which Luther himself repudiated; but on the other hand Luther was so bitterly opposed to both of them, because he supposed that they recognized in the sacrament nothing but empty signs, without the real presence of Christ. There is much truth in this statement, no doubt; and their differences were only those that earnest men, situated as they were, might reasonably be expected to entertain.

The conference began on October 2d, 1529, in the castle, which stands on a commanding height overlooking Marburg. Many interested friends were present, but the discussion was mainly conducted by Zwingli and Œcolampadius on one side, and Luther with Melanchthon on the other. When they met in the common hall Luther took a piece of chalk and wrote upon the table cloth the words, in Latin: "This is my body." Zwingli maintained that the meaning of that Scripture was: "This signifies my body." The discussion turned on the meaning of the little word " is," and neither one seemed able to bring the other over to his view. Luther kept

repeating the words, "This is my body," and
Zwingli kept asking him if he meant that Christ's
body and blood were locally there, in the bread
and wine. The latter claimed that Christ spoke
in the same sense that He used in the words : " I
am the vine;" that there is a figure of speech in the
passage, as in the expressions : " John is Elias,"
" The rock was Christ." Luther admitted that
there are figurative expressions in the Bible like
those mentioned, but he insisted that the words,
" This is my body," were to be received literally.

There was but little hope of an entire agreement between the reformers, for they differed,
just where a difference has ever since existed
between good men, in their views of the Lord's
Supper. Zwingli brought forward the words of
our Saviour in John 6th, and 63: "The flesh pro-
fiteth nothing ; the words that I speak unto you,
they are spirit, and they are life." He also quoted
the words of the Creed: " He ascended into
heaven." Also, that He was to be like His
brethren in all things, sin excepted ; and added :
" He therefore cannot be in several places at
once."

Zwingli farther quoted, in Greek, the words :
" Made himself of no reputation, and took upon
him the form of a servant." Luther interrupted

him with : "Read it to us in Latin or in German, not in Greek." Zwingli said : "Pardon me ; for twelve years past I have made use of the Greek Testament only." Luther continued : "Most dear sirs, since my Lord Jesus Christ says, 'This is my body,' I believe that His body is really there." "How, then," asked Zwingli, "can you avoid re-establishing popery ? You say Christ's body is there ; but if it is in a place, it is in heaven, whence it follows it is not in the bread." Luther said : "I have nothing to do with mathematical proofs. As soon as the words of consecration are pronounced over the bread, the body is there, however wicked be the priest who pronounces them."

It was evident, at last, to all that were present, that a full agreement was not to be hoped for; and the reformers on both sides were exhorted to shake hands and separate in friendship, agreeing to differ in their views of the doctrine under discussion. Zwingli came forward and frankly, as his habit was, held out his hand, which, at first, Luther refused to take. This brought tears into the eyes of Zwingli, who had not expected such conduct on the part of Luther; and the Landgrave added his earnest exhortation that they should separate as friends. Ac-

counts differ as to the final result in regard to
the hand shaking. Daubigne says: "Luther
then advanced towards the Swiss, and said, 'We
consent, and I offer you the hand of peace and
charity.' The Swiss rushed in great emotion
towards the Wittenbergers, and all shook hands."

Some resolutions of concord were then drawn
up, the last words of which are as follows:
"And although we have not been able now to
agree, as to whether the true body and blood of
Christ are corporeally present in the bread and
wine, yet one party ought to exercise Christian
charity towards the other, as far as each conscience can possibly allow it, and both parties
ought to beseech God fervently, to lead us by
His Spirit to a right understanding. Amen."

The following, given by Hottinger, as a letter
written by Luther to a friend, also throws light
upon this historic interview: "They," the
Swiss, "promised with many words, they would
yield this much to us, that the person of Christ
was really, though spiritually, present in the
Holy Supper, if we would only esteem them
worthy of the name of brethren, and in this way
feign a reconciliation. Zwingli begged it with
tears in his eyes before the Landgrave and all
present, while he added: 'There are no men

with whom I would rather be united than with
the Wittenbergers.' They never could endure
my saying: 'You have another spirit than we.'
Finally we granted so much, that it might stand
at the conclusion of the article, not indeed that
we were brethren, but that we would not withdraw from them our love, which is due even to
an enemy." That Luther himself was pained at
the result of the interview is evident from another statement made, as Christoffel informs, us in
writing, on his departure from Marburg: "I
crawled liked a worm in the dust, and so tormented was I, by the devil, that I thought never
more to have seen nor wife, nor child; I, the
comforter of distressed souls, was without comfort."

Daubigne gives the following reflection, on
the close of the conference: "If Luther had
yielded, it might have been feared that the
church would fall into the extreme of rational-
ism; if Zwingli, that it would rush into the extreme of Popery. It is a salutary thing for the
church that these different views should be entertained; but it is a pernicious thing for indi-
viduals to attach themselves to one of them, in
such a manner as to anathematize the others.
If it is maintained that a wicked priest operates

this real presence of Christ by three words, we
enter the church of the Pope. Luther appeared
sometimes to admit this doctrine, but he has
often spoken in a more spiritual manner; and
taking this great man in his best moments, we
behold no more than an essential unity and a
secondary diversity in the two parties of the
reformation." It is pleasant to look at the
matter in this light, and here we leave the subject of the controversy, only adding a word as
to Zwingli's real views of the Sacrament as we
find them expressed in his writings.

In the eighteenth article of his famous sixty-
seven theses, he says: "Christ offered Himself
once, and is forever a permanent compensative
sacrifice for the sins of all believers: Whence
we conclude that the mass is not a sacrifice, but
a commemoration of a sacrifice, and a seal of the
redemption which He has procured for us." In
the confession which he sent Francis I, shortly
before his death, he writes: "We believe that
Christ is truly present in the Lord's Supper;
yea, we believe that there is no communion
without the presence of Christ." And again:
"We believe that the true body of Christ is
eaten in the communion in a sacramental and
spiritual manner by the religious, believing,

and pious heart, as also St. Chrysostom taught."
Zwingli also compared the sacrament to a wed-
ding ring which seals the marriage-union; and
he makes the act of communing, a confession of
the believer's faith, and an expression of gratitude for blessings received. In this he has been
instrumental in voicing the sentiment of the
whole protestant church, nearly. Calvin indeed
emphasized the reality of the spiritual presence
of Christ at the supper; but had he been spared
to see the time of Calvin, Zwingli would, without doubt, have adopted his more elaborate
definition, for their views were not conflicting.

The conference at Marburg was now ended,
and Zwingli returned in safety to his home, to
resume his arduous duties. The pen of the reformer wrought marvellously. His published
books give evidence of the industry with which
he labored. They consist of four folio volumes
containing the following works,—Articles of
Faith.—An Exhortation. to the whole State
of Switzerland.—A Supplication to the Bishop
of Constance.—Of the Certainty and Purity of
God's Word.—On the Fathers.—Institution for
Youth.—A Good Shepherd.—Of Justice, Divine
and Human.—Of Providence.—A Treatise on
Baptism—On Original Sin. On True and False

Religion.—An Epistle to the Princes of Germany.—On the Lord's Supper.—On Christian Faith.—Commentaries on Genesis, Exodus, Isaiah, Jeremiah, and The Psalms from the Hebrew and Latin. His works on the New Testament are, History of our Saviour's Passion.—Notes on the four Gospels, the Epistles to the Romans, Corinthians, Philippians, Colossians, Thessalonians and Hebrews; the Epistle of James, and the first Epistle of John. For the most part they were written in German, and afterwards translated into Latin.

We can but wonder how, amid all his other duties, he found time to produce this vast amount of literature. He once complained: "No man is more unfortunately situated than I for writing books. It is owing to the evil nature of the times. For it drags me out, who would rather keep silence and lie concealed, and compels me to write, while it obstinately refuses me leisure to do the work, and the years requisite for the employment of the file." He sees the hand of Providence in all this, however, and would be willing to have all his works pass into oblivion, if he could only get the Holy Scriptures into general circulation, and use. During all this time he preached incessantly, besides attending conferences at Bern and elsewhere in which the chief labor of formulating the doctrines of the Reformed fell upon him. At the same time, he went forward with his pastoral work in Zurich, received a multitude of visitors, and attended to the training of his own children.

His heart was with his family, while his mind was at work for the cause he had espoused. This we see from a letter which he wrote while at Bern. "Grace and peace from God, dearest wife. I praise God that he hath given you a happy recovery. He will grant us grace to bring up our children according to his will. Pray to God for me, and for us all. Greet for me all our children, especially comfort Margaretha in my name." This shows us what a kind heart dwelt in Zwingli. Christoffel says: "This man, who investigated with such penetration, and zeal, the sacred depths in which truth conceals itself from the unconsecrated eye; who wrought in the vineyard of the Lord with the lofty ardor of an apostle—this man we often find, in his hours of recreation, at the cradle of his little one, singing children's songs to the accompaniment of the lute, or some other instrument, which he knew."

This love to his family should endear him to every heart.

CHAPTER XVI.

DEATH AT CAPPEL.

A GLANCE at almost any picture, representing the city of Zurich, will afford the reader a view of the water-front, where the strong current of the Limmat sweeps onward towards the Rhine. A few steps away from the quay which borders the right bank, and, as already described, resting on the side of the terrace, stayed by the ancient buttresses built before the Reformation period, stands the cathedral in which Zwingli preached. A little farther from the river bank we may see the house in which he lived. It is a plain, but substantial structure, having its gable towards the church, with two stories and attic, in the latter of which there are two windows, while in each of the lower stories there are four windows; so that, by this mark, the house is easily identified. A large and pleasant garden adjoins the house on the south side, giving the place a home-like, and inviting, ap-

174

pearance. Here it was that Zwingli dwelt in
joy, with his household, delighting to entertain
the many guests, who came to him for temporal
and spiritual comfort.

Many were the afflicted pastors that fled to
this refuge, when the persecutions grew threat-
ening and the outlook for the Reformed was
gloomy, and the heavy hand of the enemy lay
upon them. Those who came, like poor Myconius,
who before this had been thrust out of Lucerne,
were sure of a hearty welcome, and besides
were refreshed and encouraged by the cheerfulness of the great Reformer, who, up to the time
of which we are now about to write, was noted
for his wonderful courage and hope. He used
to say: "Whoever is filled with the Spirit of
God, is ever on the alert to do something for
the benefit of his fellow-men, is unwearied in
every good work, and rather is fearful that he
may do less than he ought. We must therefore be active and fervent in our labors, not
sleepy nor slothful; we must not withdraw
from the divine calling, nor take holiday, but
be ever on the alert, and bear a ready hand to
the work."

This injunction to be diligent in labor, the
Reformer himself fully exemplified in his own

life. Of naturally a strong physical constitution, frugal in diet, as in his youth still using milk and the other products of the dairy, as his chief articles of food, he was enabled to undergo great strains of labor and anxiety. When in 1526, Œcolampadius, and Haller were disputing with Dr. Eck, in the council at Baden, Zwingli who, remained in Zurich, did not retire to bed for six weeks, being occupied the whole night, in preparing answers to the charges of the papists. Only the strong frame of a mountaineer could support nature under the heavy pressure that lay upon him. His home was indeed his castle; there he found loving hearts and helpful counsel, and from thence he went forth, with renewed strength, to his appointed work, in the pulpit, the council, and the pastorate.

But as we have intimated, a change in the posture of affairs at Zurich was now at hand. The treaty made with the five papal cantons at the first war of Cappel was extremely distasteful to the latter. They saw that the Reformation was steadily gaining ground. Zwingli, its great leader, was indefatigable in his efforts, and was winning many hearts not only in Zurich, but also in Bern, and in St. Gaul, and in the regions surrounding the Toggenburg. It was evident that the five cantons were preparing for another warlike demonstration. The Reformed looked to a union of those who were favorable to their views. Zwingli was especially in accord with this plan.

Slanderous reports were now freely circulated throughout the land by the papists, and this was done while the treaty was in full force that no abusive language should be used. It was said: 'Zwingli is a thief, a murderer, an arch-heretic,' and that it was the duty of the five cantons to sweep away the entire body of Reformers from the face of the earth. Against the pastor of Zurich the fierceness of the intended persecution was aimed. One pensioner said: "I shall have no rest, until I have thrust my sword up to the hilt in the body of this impious wretch." Threats were followed by deeds of violence. The five cantons pursued all among those who loved the Word of God. They flung them into prison, imposed fines upon them, brutally tormented them, and mercilessly expelled them from their country. It was evident that this state of affairs could not last much longer.

The Bernese and Zurichers, now acting in
12

concert, while casting about them for some means to check these outrages, were reminded that, at a former time, the five cantons had established a blockade against the Reformed. They now resolved to turn the tables, and close up their markets against the foe, until they allowed the Word of God to be freely preached, according to the treaty. Against this course Zwingli was strongly opposed. He believed that by this means many worthy people would suffer hardship, that the five cantons would only be aggravated to adopt more extreme measures and that thus the difficulties of the situation would be greatly increased. He was rather in favor of active measures ; for even making a declaration of war, and pushing the issue, that he now saw was inevitable, to a conclusion at once.

But the pastor of Zurich, whose advice in matters of religion had been so widely honored, found that he had entered a different field when he assumed to give counsel in matters of state. The measures of the blockade having been agreed upon, it became his duty to announce the fact from his pulpit. Daubigne says : " On the following Sunday Zwingli appeared in his church, where an immense crowd was waiting

for him. His piercing eye easily discovered the
dangers of the measure, in a political point of
view, and his Christian heart deeply felt all its
cruelty. His soul was overburdened, his eyes
downcast. After the regular services were
concluded, he proceeded to read the resolutions
which had been adopted, declaring that the
Waldstetters were to be excluded from their
markets. But he immediately added his protest: 'Men of Zurich! you deny food to the
five cantons, as to evil-doers: well! let the blow
follow the threat, rather than reduce poor innocent creatures to starvation. If, by not taking
the offensive, you appear to believe that there is
not sufficient reason for punishing the Waldstetters, and yet you refuse them food and drink,
you will force them, by this line of conduct, to
take up arms, to raise their hands, and to in-
flict punishment upon you. This is the fate that
awaits you.'" A sad but true prophecy, as the
sequel proved, and one that would involve the
Reformer in its painful result.

The difficulty of enforcing the orders given
for the blockade may be easily imagined. Whatever indignities the five cantons had heaped
upon the Reformed, it was unwise in them to
adopt this expedient for defence. The forest

cantons, Lucerne, Zug, Schwitz, Uri, and Unterwalden were bound in firm bonds to the interests of the papacy. Their territory lay between
that of Zurich and Bern; the effect of the
blockade therefore was to hem them in and cut
off their supplies, which they usually obtained
from the larger towns, like Zurich, Bern, and
Basel, all of which under the influence of
Zwingli and others, had embraced the Reformed
faith. The union of Zurich with Bern was
cemented by the conference which had been
held in the latter city early in the year 1528,
which lasted for eighteen days, and in which
Zwingli distinguished himself, both in the part
he took in the learned discussions, and in the
two famous sermons which he preached on the
occasion. From that time onward the Bernese
acted with Zurich; but in the matter of the
blockade, the greatest burden of defence would
fall upon the latter, while the former had been
the means of bringing it about.

The measures of the blockade were now en-
forced; the Reformed closed their markets
against the five cantons, allowing them to receive neither corn nor wine, salt, iron nor steel,
until they should allow the Gospel to be preached
among them without persecution. When the

wagons of the people of the five cantons, were driven towards the large towns, they were stopped at the border of the canton, unloaded, upset, and turned into barricades for soldiers. The year previous had been one of great scarcity in the forest cantons, and the Sweating-sickness had broken out among the people; and now, worst of all, their supplies were cut off by the very cantons against whom they had held a bitter grudge, since the peace of Cappel. The people of Schwitz, appeared openly with pine-branches in their hats, the old form of a declaration of war. Their allies were everywhere taking down their halberds and sharpening them for their intended bloody work. Recruiting went briskly forward, forces were mustering, and tidings were borne by each new comer to Zurich, that the war would soon begin.

And what preparations are the people making for defence? Life went on as usual at Zurich; the people seemed to be at ease, and the council payed no heed to the alarming tidings which came to them from beyond the mountains. Zwingli went forward with his daily labors. He preached at the regular hours; he visited the sick, and neglected none of his usual duties. The early morning hours he devoted specially

to prayer and the study of the Scriptures, till
the hour arrived which summoned him into the
church to preach, or to give the lecture in the
hall of the Academy. In the evening, as usual,
he was engaged with his extensive correspondence; now encouraging the people of St. Gaul,
who had taken a noble stand for the truth, casting out all the images from their houses of worship; or writing to those who sought spiritual
counsel and comfort. But the spirit of former
days had fled from him. The sound of music is
now seldom heard in his apartments. He pores
over the gloomy Prophecies of Jeremiah, as if
he found something in those lamentations suited
to the distracted condition of his own times and
country.

One night he went out, with some friends, to
confer with Parson Bullinger at Bremgarten.
During this nocturnal conference, three town
councillors were stationed as sentinels before
the parsonage. Before daylight Zwingli took
his way homeward; his mind was filled with a
presentiment of his approaching death. Bathed
in tears, he said at parting: "O my dear
Henry, may God protect you. Be faithful to
our Lord Jesus Christ and His church." And
so they parted. The advice seemed most timely,

in view of the fact that Bullinger became his successor in Zurich. The Reformer once, in those days, gave vent to his feelings in his pulpit, in the following language : " I see that the most faithful warnings cannot save you ; you will not punish the pensioners of the foreigner. They have too firm a support among us! A chain is prepared—behold it entire—it unrolls link after link—soon they will bind me with it, and more than one pious Zuricher with me. . . It is against me they are enraged! I am ready ; I submit to the Lord's will. But these people shall never be my masters !"

The Zurichers still continuing passive, Zwingli, after a long struggle with himself, and earnest prayer, handed in his resignation to the council, stating that he had labored among them for eleven years, but that he could not now arouse them to a sense of their common peril, and therefore asked them to relieve him of his pastorate. This they refused to do ; and the Reformer, with his characteristic sense of honor, would not voluntarily leave them in the time of trial. A messenger now arrived from Lucerne, with the tidings that the standard of battle had been planted in the great square. This was the rallying point for all the soldiers of the five

cantons. A hasty proclamation was sent forth
to the effect that the attacks made upon the
treaties, the discord sown throughout the Confederation, and especially the refusal to sell them
provisions, was the cause of the warfare. Hardly
had the messengers, bearing these despatches,
departed, before the army was put in motion.
Upon entering the free districts, the soldiers entered the churches and observed that the images
had been removed; this aroused their anger,
and they pillaged and plundered without limit,
especially in the houses of the pastors. At the
same time, the division that was to form the
main army marched upon Zug, thence to move
upon Zurich.

The Zurichers were under a complete delu-
sion; the members of the council simply said,
when the first news of the war came, that the
five cantons were only making a little noise to
frighten them. But when the enemy appeared
at Zug refugees hastened to Zurich with their
woful tidings. Now the whole city was
aroused. A straggling army was - hastily
brought together; a few energetic men pushed
on to the old battle field, on the border line of
their territory, at Cappel. This had been the
seat of an ancient convent, hence the name

Cappel, or Chapel. Citizens with members of the council were seizing their arms; a reign of terror had commenced, and a sudden attack upon the defenceless city was feared. It was needful that men should go on towards Cappel, that the blood-thirsty cantoners might be turned back. A horse, ready saddled, stood pawing the ground, and champing his bit, in front of the Parsonage in Zurich. He is to bear his master away to the battle-field. At the orders of the council, and in keeping with the old Swiss customs, he must attend the little army as chaplain, that he may cheer up the men, and give comfort to the dying. We have seen that Zwingli was without any hope that the expedition would be successful. He went forth from a sense of duty, under the presentiment that he would never see his dear wife and children on earth again.

Poor Anna Zwingli, had a double portion of sorrow to bear that day. Her early life had been filled with sadness, but in later years, she had been happy in the home of her husband, with her little ones growing up around her. But to-day that sweet cup of domestic bliss is embittered by fears and anxious forebodings. Her husband, her son Gerold, and her brother are all hastening away to the battle-field, she will never see them more until they meet in the land where there are no partings. Zwingli took down his armor from the wall; he bade his weeping wife and children farewell, and as if riding to his martyrdom, as he was, without enthusiasm, without hope, he followed, with the little army, along the windings of the Sihl, up towards the top of the Albis.

When on the way, if any one spoke to Zwingli, he was found firm in faith : he did not conceal the presentiment that he should never see his church or family again. There was but little enthusiasm on the part of the troops either. It was rather the march of a funeral procession than of an army, except that all was disorder and confusion. Along the whole route, some ten or twelve miles distance from Zurich, messengers came running in breathless haste urging them to come to the assistance of their brethren.

When they were half way to Cappel, and climbing up the steep side of Mt. Albis, they heard the report of the first shot fired by the enemy. It had passed over the convent of Cappel; and was the signal for immediate action. This nerved the men to renewed effort; they pushed on, overburdened with armor, dragging the artillery, panting, fainting, leaning against the trees for a moment's rest, and appearing to be stragglers rather than soldiers.

Once on the summit, they paused a moment to take breath, and look down into the region where the battle was already raging; to many of them it was to be a field of death.

Here the little army halted for counsel; some were for delaying until more recruits should come in. But the advanced guard of the Zurichers, were already engaging the enemy, within their sight, having only a handful of men while the enemy were present in overwhelming numbers. Zwingli said: " How can we stay calmly upon these heights, while we hear the shots that are fired at our fellow-citizens? In the name of God I will march towards our warriors, prepared to die in order to save them." This is indeed a critical moment! O that some Frederic the Wise were here to bear this man of God hence, even as he bore Luther away to the castle of Wartburg! But this was not to be; there was one life that all that army of the Cantons had been marshalled to extinguish, and the hour of their triumph was at hand.

The tide of battle soon swept over the place where the Reformer, and the troops of Zurich, were passing. From a dense piece of woods, near at hand, the enemy poured forth a murderous volley which swept down many Zurichers before it. Soon after this the Reformer, while he was bending over a fallen countryman to give him Christian comfort, was struck on his helmet by a stone, with such force that he was thrown to the ground. In this fact we see the importance of Zwingli having armor upon his person. Though he carried weapons of the old Swiss pattern, he did not use them. The chaplains in those times, wore armor, as chaplains now wear uniforms. He soon summoned up strength to rise again, when he received a fatal stroke from a spear. He again fell and exclaimed: " What evil is this ? They can kill the body, but they cannot kill the soul." These were his last words.

Night spread her mantle over the scene of carnage. Some prowling soldiers, discovered Zwingli lying near a pear tree, against which his body partly leaned : his hands were firmly clasped, his lips moved in prayer, while his eyes were directed heavenward: " Will you confess, shall we fetch a priest ?" they cry to

CAPPEL.

him. He only shakes his head. "Then call upon the mother of God, and the blessed saints, in your heart," they cry. The dying man heeds them not. The soldiers uttered a volley of oaths over the fallen man, saying: "No doubt you are one of those heretics of Zurich." One man, being anxious to know who he was, and as it was already growing dark, stooped down, raised his head and turned it toward the camp-fire, which had been kindled near by, and then dropping it heavily, exclaimed, "I think it is Zwingli"! An officer, named Captain Bockinger, from Unterwalden, a papist, and a pensioner, upon hearing the name Zwingli, hurried to the spot. He said: "Zwingli! that vile heretic, that rascal, that traitor! Die then, obstinate heretic!" and suiting the action to the word, he struck him with his sword, inflicting a fatal wound.

Thus on October, 12th, 1531, the spirit of that noble man took its flight to that God whose service had been, for years past, his delightful employ. The morning dawned. The victors spread themselves upon the field to gloat over the havoc they had wrought. They found the remains of many noble men who had died in the vain attempt to turn away danger from their homes.

Some twenty pastors of the Reformed lay
stretched upon the field, among the slain. At
last the conquerers reached the pear-tree where
lay the lifeless body of Zwingli. " Immediately
the drums beat to muster; the dead body was
tried, and it was decreed that it should be quar-
tered for treason against the Confederation, and
then burnt for heresy. The executioner of Lucerne carried out the sentence. Flames con-
sumed Zwingli's disjointed members; the ashes
of swine were mingled with his : and a lawless
multitude rushing upon his remains, flung them
to the four winds of heaven." Some kind-
hearted Reformers, it is said, have planted
young pear-trees on the spot where Zwingli fell;
as each successive tree grew old, therefore, a
new tree was ready to take its place, and a
" Zwingli pear-tree," is found here at the present time. Also a metal plate is inserted in the
rock near by, and at the road-side, bearing a
German and Latin inscription, descriptive of
Zwingli's death. Yet he has a better monument
than this in the affection of many Christian
hearts.

After some time of warlike demonstration
between the two armies, following that bloody
contest on the 12th of October, negotiations

were entered into looking to a final peace. On the 16th of November, the following articles were adopted. "The Reformation shall be guaranteed in Zurich, and all her immediate dependencies, as well as in other places where it has been received; yet all those, who may wish to return to the mass, or to prove by a new vote, which is the prevailing party, shall be at liberty to do so. Church property was to be divided according to the census, and Zurich pledged herself to abstain from any farther intervention, where she had no claim to rule." And so ended the second war of Cappel.

Poor Anna Zwingli, when the tidings were borne to her of her husband's death, sank down upon her knees, and with her weeping children around her called upon the God of the widow, and the fatherless. Her son, her brother, and her brother-in-law had also been slain. But she knew where to turn in her overwhelming affliction; she trusted in Christ.

Zwingli was not forty-eight years of age when he thus laid down his life for his country, and for his faith in God. He still lives, in the affection of all those who long to see the human mind freed from the bonds of ignorance, and the soul freed from the shackles of spiritual

despotism. Wherever the religion of Protestantism is spread over the earth, there will
men admire the learning, the loftiness of soul,
the courage and the piety of Ulric Zwingli.

> " Servant of God, well done!
>   Rest from Thy loved employ;
> The battle fought, the victory won,
>   Enter Thy Master's joy!
>
> The voice at twilight came;
>   He started up to hear;
> A mortal arrow pierced his frame;
>   He fell, but felt no fear.
>
> His spirit with a bound
>   Left its encumbering clay:
> His tent, at sunrise, on the ground
>   A darkened ruin lay.
>
> The pains of death are past,
>   Labor and sorrow cease,
> And life's long warfare closed at last,
>   His soul is found in peace.
>
> Soldier of Christ, well done!
>   Praise be Thy new employ;
> And while eternal ages run,
>   Rest in Thy Saviour's joy!"